The

Warping

Full Disclosure One

Ellis Logan

An Earth Lodge® Publication
Roxbury, Connecticut

Published in the U.S.A. by Earth Lodge®
Cover Design by Maya Cointreau

ISBN 978-1-944396-41-1

The Sun, the Sky,
The Moon, the Stars.
Don't forget just who you are.

- The Sky People

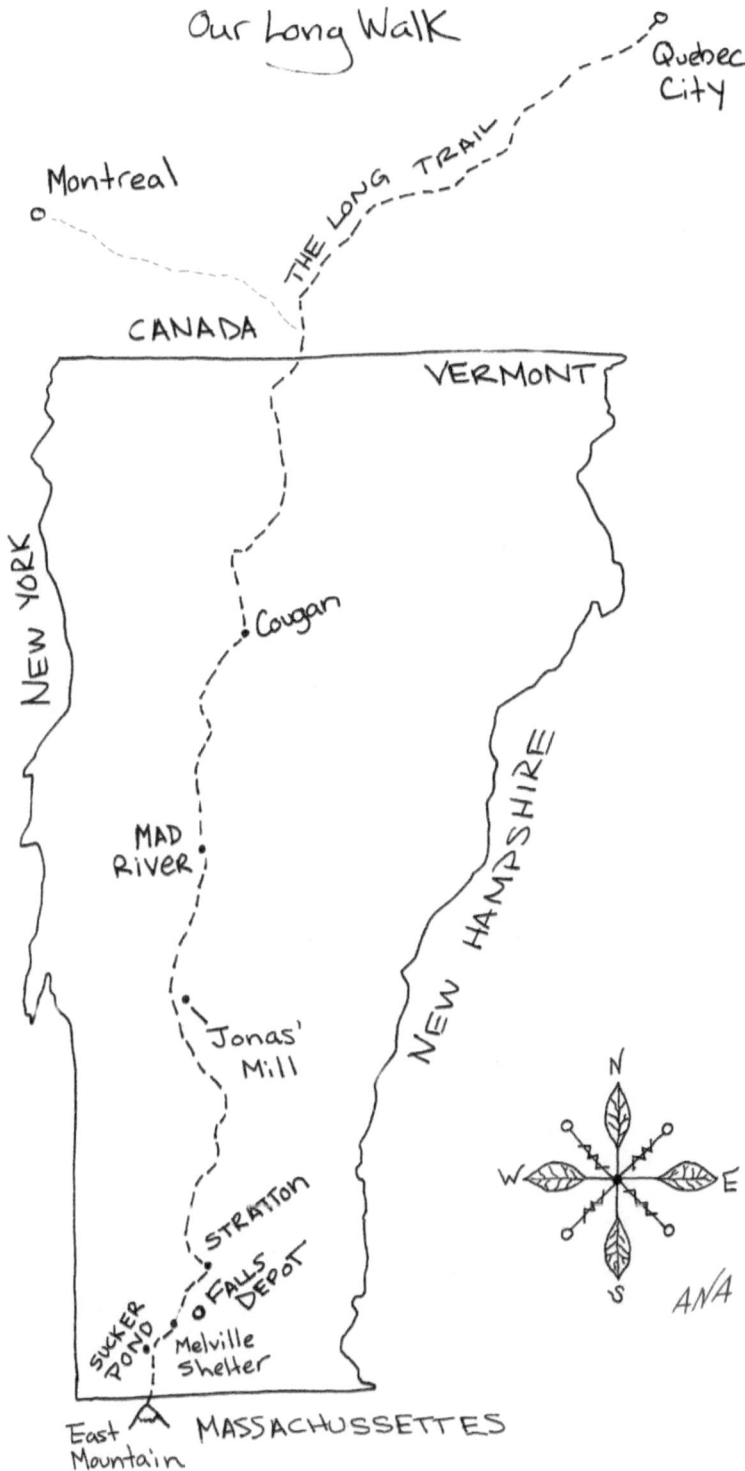

Prologue

A thousand feet above the ground, the young woman sat hidden in the Tree of Life.

She thought of her friends far below in the seven surrounding golden towers, watching. Waiting for her to take action. What should she do?

Among the chatter of the birds a new song was taken up.

"They are coming! The Shadows. They are here! Run. Hide!"

Sure enough, she could hear the low hum of the Dark fae's vehicles approaching, surrounding the great tree below.

What could she do?

She placed her hands over a well-worn knot in the bark of the tree, and prayed. She sent all her heart into the tree, furiously trying to connect, to access its core. She sent healing. She sent love. She sent wonder and respect.

At first, she felt nothing. Then, a stirring. A glimmer of acknowledgment. A slow awakening.

And then, she was consumed. Consumed with knowledge. She could see the Ancient home of her people, the land from whence the tree had come, the city where its mother had grown and shed its seed. She watched the great ship flee the world, travel the stars, and choose a place not far from a golden sun to create a new home. She saw the seed unfurling; the tree growing almost as if overnight; the red sun, Anansanna, awakening. The terraforming of the Earth, the populating of the world, above and below, on the surface and deep within around the Tree. She saw the humans breeding, growing in numbers, and the fae retreating below the earth into Aeden to allow the younger species time to evolve.

She saw the Divide with the Shades, the Dark fae who yearned to conquer the humans, to rule the world as a superior race. Oh, that was so painful, the sadness the tree had felt to see its beloved lights splitting apart into darkness. The young woman experienced it all. Through Anansanna, through the sun, the tree created life, anchored it, blessed it. Even when there was pain, even when there was sorrow, the tree lived on. But it had been so, so sad and lonely of late. It felt the pain of the world it had created and had been calling for help.

For the tree could not work alone. Just as it anchored the red sun, it needed someone to help fix its attention, to guide it, to co-create a new world. It could not be done alone. Fae and tree had to work together, as they had always done.

It felt the girl's own sorrow and perseverance, the love in her heart, and it recognized her instantly. She was its heart. The soul that was needed in the recipe for creation.

Her consciousness grew to fill the tree from the tip of its boughs to the depth of its roots, connecting everything so that tree and girl became as one organism. Together, they formed a hive of empathy, of love and trust.

The bond was complete. The energy filled the girl, filling her, fueling her. The tree lifted its limbs to cradle her, to hold her in position. She couldn't have fallen, anyway. Her hands were glued to the knot on the tree, immovable.

Light exploded from her eyes and she screamed, throwing back her head as she poured all her healing energy into the tree, to heal the small sun hidden within the center of the earth. To heal the rift of light and dark and re-forge the world.

The sun flashed, a pulse of blue light escaping from the red, a massive solar flare sending newly awakened ions at the speed of light through all of Aeden, from the earth's core to all peoples far and wide.

In that moment, she was one with everything. She was able to feel the leader of the Shades and his minions fall to their knees, weeping with joy as the veil of darkness dissolved around them. No longer were they separate from the light. She saw wars around the world stop in their tracks, weapons laid down as if they were poison. Abusers prostrating themselves to beg forgiveness. Executioners lowering their swords.

Hate fled the world as love rushed in. Anger turned to compassion, guilt turned to acceptance.

In an instant, there was peace on earth.

Fear was banished from all people's hearts. The world was reforged. Awakened.

Greed became a thing of the past, since there was no "us versus them" mentality. Within several years, most illnesses were cured, the world unanimously transitioned to renewable energy sources, and nature began to recover from the harm of man.

Relationships became equal, honest and open. People started working on what interested them, when and where they wanted, stimulating creativity in ways no one could have foreseen.

The borders of Aeden opened, allowing free communication between fae and humans. No longer did the fae segregate themselves deep within the hollow earth, beneath the world of men. Light fae returned above below, back to Midgard, to the outer world. Humans seeking knowledge of the past, for the present and future, were allowed to explore the realm of Aeden deep within the earth. Allowed to see the red sun with their own eyes, given leave to tour the city of Valhalla with its Tree of Life, to visit the vibrant artist colony of Elysielle, to travel the plains of Roumkivara, to shop in the golden cities of Sibollae and Aurin, or to ski the mountain ranges of Niflhelf.

Technology was shared and new horizons opened up above, below, and in space. A colony quickly sprang up on the Moon, and within a decade plans were laid out to terraform Mars, a vast project that would take fifty more years to complete.

With the amped up ions pumping through the world, everything changed, including the humans. Bigotry, misogyny, sexism and racism became relics of the past. More and more young adults awakened every day with elemental powers, and children and babies exhibited signs of increased intuition, stamina and regenerative capabilities. Life spans were predicted to grow, the human race slowly but surely shifting towards becoming fae, who had always lived hundred, if not thousands, of years.

It seemed that the only thing separating the species really had been a degree of light.

Things would change for the fae, too. Faelings would access their powers at Ascensions, not Choosings, since the only choice now would be the Light. More and more fae would mingle in the human world, falling in love, mating and bringing both species even closer together. More fae would access old, rare and forgotten abilities. Talking to animals. Hearing the song of the sun. Flying.

4

And the girl? She enjoyed the ride. Her responsibilities as the Heart of Life ended that day on the Tree of Life, when her tattoo burned and the red sun on her ankle disappeared.

She still has a ring of blue arrows above her foot, a constant reminder to always be Tyr-wise and Tyr-brave. A lesson she has tried to teach her children, her students, and all she meets. Because who knows when a divide might happen again, when another Heart of Life will arise and need to save the day.

Chapter 1

Thirty years after The Flare...

Lightning flashed across the sky and thunder rolled on the air, thrumming through my body. The clouds had darkened ominously, and I knew I needed to get back home.

To be honest, I should have returned hours ago. The family was waiting. Jade wouldn't kill me, but she would give me one of her ever-withering glares, I was sure of it.

I buried my face in Ayita's pale white mane, and stroked her neck, urging her on with my thoughts.

"Faster, girl." I didn't want to go, but the rain would start falling any moment. I couldn't put it off any longer. "Take us home."

Ayita obliged without breaking her stride, leaving the meadow and heading into the deep woods near our home, following a wide path my father kept clear for riding. Well, mostly clear.

Ayita gathered her legs and vaulted over a large oak that had fallen across the trail three years ago during an ice storm. Another flash of lightning glimmered above the forest canopy, and rain began to fall. The leaves overhead shielded us from the worst of it, and my steed did not slow. Ayita was used to running in the wet. She'd grown up among the waterfalls and plateaus of Roumkivara, just one of the many incredibly fast and surefooted green-eyed unicorns prized by the riders in the area.

Even though the rains had just reached us, the river was already running high, fed by the runoff upstream. As we approached, I could see large branches being swept along the cresting waves.

Not a good day for a swim.

Luckily, I had Ayita, and wouldn't have to cross the twenty foot gap on my own. Where normal horses would have slowed, Ayita increased her speed, her strong, solid limbs bunching imperceptibly as she suddenly left the ground.

And we were flying.

If you'd never seen a unicorn move before, you wouldn't believe we could possibly make it. But fleet, as they liked to call themselves, weren't fully governed by regular laws of gravity. Incredibly strong, stockier than modern day horses, a fully-grown fleet could easily jump thirty and forty foot divides. Ayita was still young, and would probably always weigh in on the smaller side. Like me. But she could still outjump any horse.

We landed lightly on the other side and continued on, the lights of my house in the distance shining through the trees.

Almost home.

In just a few minutes, I'd be surrounded by family and friends, some I hadn't seen since my Ascension the year before.

I should have been happy. Most people would have been happy.

I wasn't most people.

No, I was the awkward, bumbling daughter of two of the most amazing people in the entire world.

You think I'm exaggerating.

I'm not.

My mom saved the world. Literally. Saved. The. World.

She had prophecies written about her thousands of years ago. The Ancients sang songs about her. About how she was the "Heart of Life" and would save or end the world. Lucky for me, and you, she saved it. Fought against the Dark, and won. Kept the world from being enslaved by a megalomaniac, basically jumpstarted the Golden Age of humanity, and cured cancer. More or less.

You get the idea.

That was before I was born, of course, over thirty years ago. Now she's just an archaeologist, traveling the world with my dad, looking for Ancient fae artifacts and keeping an eye on humanity.

They're the best parents a girl could ask for.

Except.

I shouldn't be complaining. You're right. Both my parents are elite fae warriors, they're funny, they're great. Honestly, my whole family is awesome. Even my brother isn't so bad, as far as brothers go. What could I have to complain about, right?

And really, I'm not. I don't complain. Like, ever. Just ask any of my friends. I know I have a really good life. So what if my active powers haven't manifested? Who cares if I'm a huge klutz and still the size of a twelve year old? Like my mom says, I'm perfect. I'm just a late bloomer.

So what if I'm the only person in my family who can't use her earth powers, take down a ninja with my bare hands or run a mile in under ten minutes?

I'm perfect.

Right?

Chapter 2

Back at the barn, I slid off Ayita's back and walked her to the open stall. No doors, locks or leads were needed when you rode a fleet. The unicorns bonded with their riders for life, and they could hear our every thought, even if most humans and fae still couldn't hear them back. They'd never run away, and they always came when needed, assuming you were within mental shouting distance. I still wasn't sure just how far that was, but I'd heard stories of fleet rescuing their riders from miles away.

I served her a scoop of grain topped with a handful of fresh berries, packed her feed basket with a sheaf of hay and gave her a quick brushing while she ate.

After a few minutes she stopped eating and nudged me.

"Yeah, yeah. Let me get you some water first."

I knew Ayita had heard my thoughts on the ride home, that she understood I was dreading going in. Ayita never had much patience for fear, though.

I filled the bucket in her stall with fresh, cold water and ran my hand along the smooth, gleaming hair on her neck while she drank. After a few long sips, she stuck her whole head in the bucket, making it overflow, and then pulled her head out, giving it a massive shake and spraying me with water.

I laughed, holding my hands up in a useless effort to avoid the drenching.

"Alright, I know. I'm going."

Ayita was still considered a juvenile by herd standards, and had the sass to match her age. My parents thought she would be a good balance for me, since I tended to let other people do the talking. Even by their standards as relative introverts, I was too quiet, too serious, too shy. I knew they worried that I wasn't happy, but honestly, I just found living up to the family legend a bit tiresome sometimes. Since I was a child, it had been obvious that I wouldn't ever be able to keep up. Somehow, the family genes for coordination and agility just hadn't been passed on to me. Now, with my earth powers remaining dormant, I thought it might be better if I just stayed out of everybody's way.

If I didn't disappoint anyone, then I couldn't disappoint myself, either.

At least, that's what I tried to tell myself.

I gave Ayita one last pat and put her brush back on the shelf by the door. A quick glance in the mirror hanging there revealed a level of disarray that was beyond my usual standards. My hair was a mess, the chin-length strands damp and wild from the ride. My mom always said I had my dad's untamable hair, even though mine was a faded shade of reddish-brown and his was a deep black. I did have green eyes, though, just as he'd had when he was young. Or so Mom said. I wouldn't know, since my entire life he'd had eyes the color of violets, a deep purple that blazed like royalty. Supposedly they'd changed just before The Flare, another side-effect of my mother's power back then.

Smudges of dirt marred my sun-kissed skin, and I imagined my clothes were as sorry looking as my face, even though I couldn't see them in the mirror. At five-foot-one, mirrors hung above my line of sight were something I'd grown used to. I wiped the dust off my face and straightened my shirt, hoping the brown of my breeches would at least hide the worst of it. Squaring my shoulders, I walked towards the house through the rain. Every light was on, and I could hear laughter and music from inside.

The party was in full swing. Maybe if I went in through the kitchen, I could go up the back stairs and slip into something more presentable. I headed around towards the kitchen porch, then cringed as the screen door banged open and two men came crashing through.

Blurred streaks of black, white and brown, the duo rolled down the stairs, twisting around each other while they wrestled, grunting and cursing. A glimmer of blue light sparked between them, coursing along the target's wet skin with a ghostly aura. The victim stiffened, a half-laugh escaping his lips as he shuddered, went limp and lay still on the wet ground.

Oh, I'm sorry. Did I say they were men? I meant boys.

The victor grinned as he disentangled himself to stand tall and lanky, handsome and darkly bronzed like a Brazilian, curly dark hair cropped short on his head.

"Khai!" I yelled, half in consternation, half in excitement. I hadn't seen him in person for almost six months, and now, here he was, blasting my brother unconscious.

"Ana! I didn't see you there." He caught me as I launched myself up into his arms and for a huge hug. "By the gods, you're soaked!"

He ran his hands up and down my back, his palms emitting the extra warmth that only an ascended fire fae could conjure. Steam rose around us, and I smiled up at him.

"As you will be, too, if we don't get you both back inside. Speaking of which, what did you do to my brother?"

"Just a little lightning tase, something my mom's been teaching me this week. She thought I was finally responsible enough to learn how to use it."

"Clearly, Claire was mistaken," I laughed.

"Oh, come on. How else was I supposed to beat Hollis?"

He had a point. The two friends had been sparring together since Khai had taken his first steps, toddling after Hollis. Seventeen months older, my brother hadn't wasted any time trying to teach Khai his place, even then. As far as I knew, this was the first time Khai had ever fully bested Hollis.

"Is he going to be okay?" I asked, walking over and feeling my brother's skin. Still warm. His heart, still beating. Through the sensitive skin of my palms, I could feel his vital energy clearly. Healthy enough.

"Oh, sure. He'll be fine. In an hour or two," Khai cackled, his short dark hair curling and glistening with rain. "I think the rain may have amped up the charge a bit." I gave him a stern look and he shook his head, having the grace to look guilty. "Okay, fine. Come on, help me get him up."

With a little help from me, Khai swung Hollis up over his shoulder and walked up the steps into the house.

I paused. So much for making a quiet entrance, I thought, fussing with my hair again. Khai turned at the door and looked at me.

"Don't worry, you look fine. Now come on. Everybody's been dying to see you."

Exactly what I was afraid of.

Chapter 3

Khai traipsed through the kitchen, Hollis' head and arms bumping along like a pale rag doll behind him. I sighed, knowing I had no choice but to follow. We walked into the living room, where everyone was standing around talking, and Khai dropped Hollis unceremoniously onto a vacant loveseat.

"What happened?" My mother rushed forward, placing her hands on Hollis' head, closing her eyes as she made the same assessment I had. Or better, maybe, because she spun on Khai. "Khai Mirro! Lightning? You tased my son? In a rain storm? Do you have any idea how dangerous that could have been? Claire!" She yelled, calling her childhood friend over. "You've been teaching Khai, I take it?"

Claire grinned over my mother's shoulder, raising one dark eyebrow as she took in Hollis' current state. "Yep."

"Hmph," my mom snorted. "Well, Khai, I hope you'll be more careful next time and mind your environment."

"Yes, ma'am. Sorry." Khai shuffled his feet and tried to look contrite, but there was no missing the gleam in his azure eyes.

She shook her head, about to say something more, but then she noticed me standing there. So much for being inconspicuous.

"Ana, darling! There you are. We were worried about you, out in the storm. I tried calling you but you never answered. Did you have a good ride?"

"Oh, yeah, um, hi everybody. Yes, it was great. I could have stayed out all evening."

"Yes, well, we're glad you didn't. Supper's almost ready. Why don't you go upstairs and put on some dry clothes?"

"Okay," I mumbled, and ducked out of the room.

Upstairs, I stripped quickly and hopped into the dry shower, a mixture of sonic pulses and light waves rendering me squeaky clean and dry in seconds. I stepped out and pulled on some dark blue linen pants and a shimmery halter top. Somehow, not only was I half-foot shorter than everyone in my family, but I had curves everywhere they didn't. It was like I was a throwback to some distant relation generations ago. If I wasn't careful how I dressed, I could wind up looking like a round plum, unlike my mom who looked great no matter what she threw on. At least the summer air was warm, despite the rain, and I didn't have to worry about figuring out layers.

I eased on some sequined slippers and ran a brush through my hair, for all the good it would do me. The reddish-brown waves just bounced back into place, curling haphazardly around my ears. I set the brush back down on my dresser, next to my Chat device. The flesh colored communications piece was designed to rest in your ear, allowing you talk with anyone, anywhere, anytime. As long as they had a Chat, that was. You could even call up a video hologram of the other person in front of you, so you could see your friend on the other line. Exactly how they did this remained a mystery to me, although Hollis had tried to explain it a thousand times. Something about sonar and 3D wave replication and blah, blah, blah.

I was so not a science girl. Give me a good book, a quiet corner, and some hot chocolate, any day. Anytime. Anywhere. That's how you made me happy.

Like I said. I was a throwback. I certainly didn't belong to this family of action-hero, parkour, martial-arts-trained archaeologists and scientists. No way.

My great-grandmother said I reminded her of her own grandmother, Skuld Norna, who had been one of the Ancient fates able to see and affect the future. I wasn't sure if that was really true, or if Kalila just said it to make me feel better, but either way I appreciated the gesture.

I left the Chat on the dresser and trudged back downstairs. My mom would have killed me if she'd known I'd gone riding without it. So what if I wasn't a kid anymore, she'd say, I'd always be her baby girl.

I guess if you'd grown up before The Flare, during the dark times when people still based most of their decisions on fear and hate, anger and greed, worrying still came easily. Even though there were no more Dark fae or even common criminals in the world, my parents remained vigilant.

Though of course, when it came to me, they worried more about me tripping and falling than any sort of evil plot endangering my life.

Chapter 4

I ducked into the dining room, hoping to take my seat without any big fanfare. As usual, things didn't work out the way I hoped.

"Ah, Ana, there you are," my mother beamed at me. "Could you do me a favor and see if you can wake your brother? I think a minute of healing will do the trick."

"Why didn't you do it?" I grumbled.

"Your mother has had enough to do getting dinner on the table and entertaining her guests. Something you could have been helping with if you'd seen fit to grace us with your presence earlier." My great-grandmother, the fearsome Jade Alvarsson, unloaded her mini lecture in a clipped Irish accent. At the end though, she smiled to lessen the blow. "Now get on with your task, and hurry back. This soup won't stay warm forever."

"It's gazpacho, Jade," my mom laughed. She'd grown up believing her grandmother was her aunt, not knowing anything other than humans even existed, and still treated the dragon like a puppy more often than not. Me? Not so much.

"Hush, child, no one asked you," Jade retorted, swatting my mother with her napkin. Everyone laughed and I fled the room.

Feet dangling over the arm of the couch, Hollis still lay in the position he'd landed. I placed a hand upon his chest and felt his lungs expand as he breathed. Matching his breath, I pulled in the energy that surrounded us, the energy I could feel flowing through all things, all the time, and poured it into my brother through the palm of my hand. Like fish to a feeding, I could feel his cells respond to the energy, vibrating faster, waking up, coming back to normal.

With a start, Hollis gasped for breath and his familiar silvery eyes, a shade darker than our mother's, blinked back at me.

"Jeez, Ana, what was that?" he complained.

"Don't look at me, I'm just bringing you back from the not-so-dead."

"Huh?"

"Khai's been practicing making lightning with Claire."

"Ah," Hollis said, sitting up slowly. "I see. Guess I'll have to be more careful from now on."

"Yeah, seems you don't know everything, after all." Hollis was an earth fae, like most of our family, and not only had those powers actually manifested, he'd also gotten the Norn gift of foresight. For years, he'd been impossible to surprise during a fight. Even my father had a hard time beating Hollis when they sparred. But apparently lightning travels faster than visions.

"Aren't you guys getting too old for this kind of stuff, anyway?" I asked.

"Never," Hollis laughed.

"I swear, Holl, sometimes I think I must be the big sister."

"If you say so, squirt," he said, tapping me on the nose like a kitten. I hated it when he did that, almost as much as I hated being called squirt.

"You suck." I pushed him back on the couch and marched away to the sound of my brother cracking up. I ignored him and went back to the table, sitting down in a huff.

"Where's your brother?" my dad asked.

"Laughing himself into an early grave," I grumbled.

"Hollis!" my father bellowed with a gleam in his violet eyes. "Get yourself in here, now."

A moment later my brother ambled into the room with a lazy grin, so reminiscent of my dad in every way except for a missing dimple and my mom's gray eyes.

"You didn't tell me dinner was on, squirt," he said as he passed my seat and ruffled my hair.

I ignored him and took a long draught of water. I'd get him back. Eventually.

Okay, not really. Revenge wasn't really my style, and it's not like I could blast him with my amazing power to... heal. Yeah. Right. Not an option. Besides, even if he was an arrogant, better than perfect, infinitely capable ass, I kind of loved the jerk.

Still, as he took his seat between Claire and Rose, two of my mom's oldest friends, I mouthed the words at him, "You're dead."

Because that's what siblings do.

I started to reach for the bread but stopped at a nudge from Khai. Looking around, I noticed no one had started eating yet. Oh, right. Grace.

My dad smiled at me. "Now that we're all here, I'd like to say how happy I am to have everyone with us. It's been too long since we all gathered under one roof."

"Yeah, when was the last time? Beltane?" Hollis wondered.

"No, Christmas," Rose answered. "Claire and Jade missed Beltane, remember?"

"No, Druid, I missed Christmas," my grandfather, Flynn, mused. "Remember? Had that broken leg back in December."

"I told you, you should have come let me heal it," my mom admonished her father-in-law.

"Right, Dad, Siri," my father interrupted them and steered the conversation back on course, "as I said, it's been a long time. Too long. I'm so glad you were all able to make the trip out for Ana's graduation tomorrow. Rose, I hope we'll get to see Maris there, too."

"She's planning on it."

"It's a shame she had to rush off to the Keltie's for the foaling," my father said, referring to the farm up the road from ours. Rose's wife, Maris, was a country vet with a knack for herbalism, and birthing season always kept her busy. "Now, I know you're all hungry, so I'll get on with it."

He reached out to join hands with my mom and her mother, Frederika, on either side. Around the table we formed an unbroken circle, hand to hand. My mom and her father Bran. Jade, Brenin Mirro and his wife, Claire. Hollis, Rose, and Flynn; my parents' mentors, Amber and Ewan – best friends, really – from when they had fought with the Light Guard. And finally, me and Khai closing the circle with Frederika.

Khai's hand felt insanely warm, even for a fire fae, and if I didn't know better I would have said I could feel the remnants of his power sparking beneath his skin. But that was probably just my imagination.

The circle complete, my father bowed his head.

"We accept this bounty today with gratitude to all that created it, the plants, the animals, the farmers and the land itself. May this food fill our hearts, bodies and minds with the radiance of Anansanna and the blessings of Life, aho-em."

"Aho-em," everyone repeated the traditional fae blessing as we released each other's hands.

Within moments, people were passing plates and striking up conversations. I took some salad as it went around and served myself a full glass of fresh-pressed orange and raspberry juice, my favorite.

I was just taking a sip when Ewan leaned towards me. "So, I hear you kids are planning some kind of big solo-hike?"

I swallowed and turned to look up at my dad's best friend. "Um, yeah. We've been planning it all spring. We're going to do the Long Trail."

"Long Trail? What's that?" he asked.

"It's the oldest long-distance trail in Vermont-"

"The whole country," Khai interjected.

"Right, all of the North American States," I said, referring to the unified trading nation comprised of every former country between Panama and Canada, plus Greenland. "The trail runs the entire length of Vermont. Our plan is to hike all the way up to Montreal, spend some time there looking for apartments before school starts. Thanks for letting us stay at your flat there, by the way."

"Anytime, you know that. So, how long will the hike take?"

"Not that long, really, maybe a month. It usually takes three weeks, but we're not in any hurry. There are a couple places we want to spend a few nights at, and some side trails we want to check out."

"Sounds fun. Just don't get lost."

"Don't worry," my dad said from across the table. "I've bought them all GPS watches for navigating."

"Can you track her with it?" Ewan asked, sounding concerned. As if I couldn't follow a trail. I mean, come on.

"What do you think?" my dad smirked. It was nice to know he had such faith in our wilderness skills.

Ewan relaxed and turned back to me, "So, who's going? Just you three?"

I nodded. "And Jules." My best friend since grade school, Jules was my polar opposite. Tall, skinny, dark as night, and a natural athlete. She'd helped me get through gym class and math, and I'd helped her write essays that didn't suck. Hiking the Long Trail was the kind of thing Jules lived for. The whole trip had been her idea, and she'd practically begged me to invite Hollis – she'd had a raging crush on my brother since middle school. Now that we'd finished fourteenth grade and were graduating high school, Jules was hoping he might actually look at her as something other than his kid sister's friend.

Good luck with that, I thought. Although as far as I knew he wasn't dating anyone – not seriously, anyways. He never seemed to date anyone long. Not that he shared stuff like that with me. Details tended to come out whenever I talked to Khai, who was sharing an apartment at school with Hollis, both of them training in engineering programs at McGill in Montreal.

"That sounds like fun, dear," Jade commented. "Hollis, I trust you will take care of the younglings."

"Hey!" Khai protested. "We're not faelings, you know. We can all handle ourselves."

Jade sighed. "I know you can, but you're not exactly adults yet, either. Jules isn't fae at all, and Ana-"

"Jules knows what she's doing. She hikes all the time," I pointed out, spearing a piece of lettuce with my fork and choosing to overlook whatever my great-grandmother had been about to say about my survival skills. "We'll be fine."

"So, when do you leave?" Rose asked brightly, and I smiled gratefully at her.

"Two days after graduation. Jules and I still have a few supplies to pick up, plus, you know, I want to make sure I get a chance to say goodbye to all my friends before I die in the woods."

"Ana!" my mom choked on her water, while Brenin and my dad both broke out laughing. I smirked at her.

"What? Everybody's thinking it." I shrugged. "I've made my peace with it."

"With dying?" Claire asked, sounding worried.

"No, with being underestimated." I rolled my eyes and looked at the bowl of strawberry, mint and basil salad in front of her. "Pass the strawberries, please?"

Looking uncomfortable, Claire pushed the bowl across the table towards me.

"Sure, here you go."

"Thanks."

An awkward silence hung in the air, and then Brenin began talking about his latest sculpture, a commission for the European Congress, and everyone's attention shifted away from me.

That was the problem, sometimes, with having a family like mine. My parents may have been raised as only children, but their friends were close like family. Claire and Brenin, Amber and Ewan, Rose and her wife Maris, they were aunts and uncles by bond, if not by blood. Khai was like a first cousin, best friend and peacemaker to both Hollis and I.

All of them my family, each one incredibly capable and dangerous in their own ways.

All of them, convinced I was not.

Sometimes, it got old. Not that the word held much meaning in our world.

Being fae, I had enough grandparent-type figures to fill a chess-board. Well, okay, maybe not quite that many. It was something my human friends didn't have to deal with, at least not yet – most of them were lucky if they'd ever met even one great-grandparent. Me? I'd met most of mine, plus a couple great-greats, and my kids would someday, too. If I ever got around to that. Longer lifespans in a utopian society meant that everyone stayed in school longer, bonded or married later – had kids, later. The same thing was happening for the humans. Soon enough, they'd get a taste of what it was like to have multiple generations breathing down your neck, judging your every move. Or not. That last part was probably just me.

My life. My luck.

Chapter 5

"You are so darn lucky," Shania sighed next to me.

"Huh?" I looked at my friend, bewildered. We were standing side by side, arranged in a vast circle on the lacrosse field, waiting for our names to be called out, checking diplomas for our name as they passed by.

"Your brother. He is so gorgeous. What I wouldn't do to have a guy like that living under my roof."

"Um, hello, gross much?" I snorted. Shania hadn't grown up around Hollis, moving to our little Vermont town of Falls Depot from the Deep South after he'd graduated. Not that it would have mattered. Girls flocked to Hollis like bees to honey. I grabbed another diploma from her hand. Hank Fesselhoff. I shut the cover and passed it on to Jules on my right.

Every year, the senior class of Union High would listen to a couple hours of speeches, then file out into the field to complete a wide circle. Names would be called out, in no particular order, and diplomas passed around. When you got yours, you were done. Graduated. When the last diploma was received, hats were thrown in the air, and friends and family standing behind you, outside the circle, would converge bearing hugs and celebratory glasses of champagne.

I knew the drill, since I'd stood on the field for Hollis' graduation three years ago, and then Khai's again the following year. The first time, I'd been excited for Hollis, and somewhat relieved to be stepping out of his shadow. The second had been bittersweet, since I knew it meant I'd be seeing a lot less of one of my best friends. But Khai and I had kept in touch, talking almost daily, so it hadn't been so different after all.

This time, it was my turn. Time to graduate fourteen years of schooling, more if you counted pre-school and kindergarten. A summer of freedom, and then seven more years of school at university. Khai and Jules had talked me into heading to McGill, too, so we'd all still be together. I hadn't told them that I was planning on spending most of my second and third years abroad at Trinity in Dublin. I knew they'd try to talk me out of it, wanting to keep me close. Everyone always wanted to keep an eye on me, as if I was helpless, a child.

I wasn't. Maybe I couldn't do what everyone else could, maybe I was smaller, or slower, but I knew I was more than they all thought. Maybe this year, I could prove it. In six months, I'd be turning twenty – legally no longer a minor, but an actual independent adult. December wouldn't just mark the end of the year, but the end of my childhood.

Shania elbowed me, bringing my attention back to the task at hand. Another diploma. Not mine.

And another. And another. Jules got hers. Then Shania. All around me, I could see more and more of the circle celebrating. Finally, my name came around. A sense of accomplishment, of relief, washed over me.

It was official. I was done. Graduated. The diplomas were still going around, fewer and farther between, but passing along, nonetheless. Finally, there was just one, going around the circle, until it was claimed. Everyone watched, silent. Expectant.

Michelle James opened the hardbacked folder, gazed at her name, and raised it above her head, triumphant. Three hundred and eighty-eight seniors yelled and cheered, and hats were launched sky-high. Jules, Shania and I hugged each other, screaming and jumping like, well, teenage girls. Then we turned and hugged our neighbors, and our families.

A muscle-bound arm came around me and I looked up into the proud face of my brother.

"Congratulations, Sis," he grinned and threw an arm around Jules, too, who smiled at him. "You, too, Jules."

"Thanks, Holl," she smiled shyly. She'd never been able to act completely normal around him. Maybe that was something else that would change now that we'd graduated. The woods were Jules' element. Surely once we'd been camping for a week or two, her confident, zany self would be able to come out and shine.

My parents came up for a hug, and then more family members. I found myself staring up at my father's childhood friend, Mialloch Airron.

"Councilman Airron! You came!" I launched myself into his open arms, his trademark stiffness melting away as they came around me.

"Of course, how could I miss my goddaughter's graduation? Congratulations, my dear Anansanna."

"Shh," I shushed him. "You know no one calls me that."

My full name had always embarrassed me, a nod to my mother's connection to the Tree of Life, to the sun that sustained us all. Another reminder of my less than humble beginnings, and everything I didn't quite live up to.

"Right, sorry, Ana." He drew back and handed me a card. "This is from my grandmother, Airmed."

"What is it?"

"Why don't you open it and see?"

I tore the envelope open and scanned its contents.

"But...it's an invitation! To study with her after we finish camping! Mom, look!"

I showed the invitation to my mother.

"That's wonderful! Airmed is still the best healer alive. There is so much you can learn from her. I always wished I had spent more time training in the healing arts with her."

"So I can go?"

"Of course, darling. You can pack a bag for Aeden and we'll have it waiting for you in Montreal when you get there, so you can go straight away." For a moment, she looked sad, her gray eyes losing some of their silvery shine. "It means I won't get to spend this last summer with you. My baby girl! I'm going to miss you so much!"

She crushed me in a hug, squeezing the air out of me with a small sob.

"Now, now," my father said, patting my mother on the back. "Loch, what have you done to my wife? I think you've broken her."

"No. I'm fine," she said, releasing me and wiping her eyes. "I'm fine, really."

"You'll come see our apartment before I start school, won't you?"

"Yes, of course I will." My mom smiled, but tears started up again in her eyes and her face crumpled. "Oh jeez, I'm sorry," she said, ducking her head into my dad's shoulder.

His arms came around her and he stroked her dark blonde hair. "Don't worry, Siri, she'll have to come home sometimes, if only to see Ayita."

"Oh, Ayita!" I exclaimed. "I don't suppose she can come with me to Aeden?"

"She could," Mialloch said seriously, "but it's quite a long trip for her."

I'd never been gone from her for so long.

"She'll have the other fleet to keep her company, and I'll make sure she has many fine runs with us, I promise." My mother looked relieved at the prospect. Now she'd have something else to take care of, something to take her mind off missing me. We all had our own unicorns, each one bonded to one of us. Kaletka for my mother, Ruis for Hollis, Moonshadow for my dad. Kaletka and Moonshadow had been the first of their kind to travel back above the hollows of Aeden to Midgard, or what we knew as the surface of the earth. They'd been hidden below, with the fae, for centuries. After their emergence, more had followed, and a wild herd of fleet now roamed the Navajo tribal lands out west. Slowly but surely, unicorns were returning to the world of men.

Shania bounced over to our group, a wide smile blazing like a warning on her face. Uh-oh. I knew that face, what it meant. There was a-

"Party at Suki's! Nine o'clock – she can go, right, Mr. Ward? Mrs. Alvarsson?"

"Yes, she can go," my father looked at me with a wicked gleam in his eye. "In fact, we insist."

Ugh. Parties were so not my thing. And my dad knew it.

"Alec," my mother said, cautioning him.

I sighed. "No, he's right. I'm going. Wouldn't miss it for the world." I plastered a fake smile on my face, determined to suck it up. Even if I hated parties, no way was I going to miss out on celebrating this important rite of passage. It was one of those things that just, I don't know, have to be done, right? I'd skipped over most high school requirements, like prom, homecoming and trying out for cheerleading. Or anything else, for that matter. But this? A party to celebrate the end of an era?

Oh yeah. I was so there.

"Did I hear someone say something about a party?" Hollis came over, Khai at his side.

"Yeah, at Suki Cree's," Shania spoke before I could stop her and I groaned.

"Aren't you a little old to be hanging out with high school kids?" I teased my brother.

"But that's just it, you're not, anymore," he said with a twinkle in his eye.

"That's right!" Shania said, bubbly as usual. "Besides, a bunch of people from the older classes will be there. You should totally come. You, too, Khai."

"Sounds great," Khai said, his lip twitching with mirth as he looked at me. He knew how I felt about parties. Even more, he knew how I felt about watching all the girls I knew trip all over my older brother. Gross.

"Perfect," my dad said, clapping my brother on the shoulder. "You can be the designated driver."

This time, it was Hollis who groaned, and I couldn't help laughing. Yeah. This was shaping up to be a really, really good day.

Chapter 6

After a festive afternoon barbecue at my house, everything was quiet, once again. Pretty much everyone had left, except for Khai, who would be riding to the party with Hollis and me, and Ewan and Amber, who were out back watching the sunset with my parents. It had been nice seeing everyone, really it had, but I'd always found myself tiring a bit around big groups of people. My mom said I was an introvert, and I just needed to make sure I got enough "me-time" when I needed it. She'd always been big on making sure I knew how to take care of myself, not just in a fight or around the house, but emotionally, on the inside.

I sprawled out on my bed, feeling very happy. It had been a great day. I'd just take a little nap, only for an hour, and then I'd get dressed. The boys were playing a new holo-game, so I knew I wouldn't be disturbed.

I watched the walls of my room darken, the waning fire of the setting sun changing them from gold, to red, to mud. The darkness bled the tension from my body, pulling me under. I closed my eyes, and drifted off to sleep. No dreams, just peace.

The next thing I saw was a glimmer of white, slashing across the room. Someone was standing in my doorway, the bright light of the hallway casting them in shadow. No, make that two someones.

"What?" I croaked.

"Get up, sleepy-head. It's fashion time!"

I'd recognize that southern twang anywhere. "Shania-"

She walked into the room, flicking on the overhead light. Jules came in next, offering me an apologetic shrug, but you could see the tiny gleam of a devil in her eyes.

"Argh." I groaned and pulled the covers over my head.

Jules ripped the blankets off me and tsked. "Nope, sorry. It's almost nine already. Time to get prettified and hit the road, so we can arrive fashionably late."

"Fine." I knew when I was beat. "I'm up."

"Great. Now you go on, sweetheart, brush your teeth and wash your face, and come on back." Shania delivered her orders in her sugar-sweet Tennessee voice as she set herself to arranging vials, brushes and various beauty potions on my desk.

I went out to my adjoining bathroom, the one I'd always shared with Hollis, and did as she asked.

"Alright, I'm yours to command," I said, returning. "Commence torture tactics."

"Ha. Ha. Very funny," Shania drawled, touching up her own flawless makeup. "Jules, will you see what you can do about her outfit, please?"

"On it."

She grabbed my hand and pulled me over to the closet.

"Alright, let's see what we can do."

"Does it really matter? I mean, everybody knows what I look like. Why do I need to get dressed up?"

"Because, most people only know what you look like when you're not trying. Shania and I, we know what you really look like. Inside and out. Why not show everybody else, okay? Go out with a bang."

"Whatever. But you know you're not going to find anything in my closet like what you're wearing."

"Thank God for that," Shania said, taking a break from curling her hair to shudder.

I laughed. Shania was a southern belle through and through, and it showed. She was dressed in a demure, yet flirty, floral dress, the top hugging her curves yet not showing too much skin, poufing out over her shoulders, while the pleated bottom was short enough that bending over or sitting down might pose a problem. Well, for me, anyways. Somehow, Shania knew just how to wear things like that and still always look and move comfortably.

Jules, on the other hand? She was the yin to Shania's yang. Dark as night, her hair in short, natural dreads, she was wearing hot pink jeans so skinny they looked painted on. A tiny white tube top left none of her athletic form to the imagination, just skimming her belly button several inches above the waist of her pants. Vibrant white eyeliner and deep fuchsia lipstick completed the edgy look.

Jules ignored her, riffling through the hangers as she spoke. "We don't want you to look like either of us. We want you to look like you."

"Well, that's good. I think I have a pair of jeans over here that'll do just that."

"Nice try, Ana. Here," she said, slapping a couple hangers against my chest and adding a pair of ankle boots to the pile. "Try these on."

I glanced at the goods and winced. "Seriously? I haven't worn this skirt in two years."

"We know," Shania and Jules said at the same time.

"Go on. Just do it," Jules implored.

I rolled my eyes, stripped down to my bra and panties, then pulled on the clothes she'd given me. The soft, multi-layered fabric of the skirt felt weightless against my thighs, so different from the jeans I usually wore year-round. Three tiers of shimmery beige chiffon over a slightly more substantial gold slip were all there was to the flouncy mini. On top, Jules had picked out a short-sleeved, pale pink light-weight sweater struck through with threads of gold. The sweater was one of my favorites, something I paired with jeans on special occasions. I'd never thought to wear it with the skirt. Well, that wasn't quite true. I'd never quite had the courage to wear something so sweet. So demure. Putting it on, I knew it would make me look just as cute and helpless as people always assumed I was.

"I don't know..."

"Oh, you look great!" Shania clapped her hands, excited. "Put on the boots! Put on the boots."

I sighed and sat down. The boots had been a present from my mom, but I'd never worn them. The tawny, kid suede boots were gorgeous. With their three-inch heels, they'd just always seemed too much for me. Too fancy for small town Vermont. Too dressy for school. As much as I hated being short, I'd always shied away from heels, not wanting to be that girl. The girl that tried too hard to be something she wasn't.

Still, I pulled them on. They fit like a glove. The soles were well-cushioned platforms, so I barely noticed the extra height of the heels. Turning in the mirror, I had to admit they looked great with the skirt, adding about a mile to my legs. Teamed with the boots, suddenly there was nothing sweet or innocent about my outfit. I looked...grownup. Smart. Confident. The pink sweater set off my hair and eyes, and the gold shimmers throughout lent a festive air to the whole ensemble.

"It's perfect," Jules said, looking on with approval. There's the Ana you've been hiding."

"I have to say, I don't entirely hate it."

"Great, then get your pretty behind over here and sit right down." Shania patted the chair at my desk, which she'd turned to face her. "I've been wanting to do this for years."

"You've done my makeup before," I said, used to her machinations. We'd had plenty of girl's nights, sleepovers when I'd allowed the two of them to doll me up.

"Yes, but not when anyone else was going to see it," she pointed out. She had me there.

"True. That's why I'm letting you do it, and not Jules."

"Hey!" Jules protested.

"Sorry, hon, what you do on yourself looks mighty fine, but when you do the same to Ana here, she looks like someone out of those old glam-rocker bands my Poppa likes to listen to. A fine face like hers needs a more delicate touch."

"Are you trying to say my face isn't fine?" Jules grumbled.

"Now you know that's not what I'm saying at all," Shania said, smoothing gold shadow over my eyes. "You're stunning and you know it. But you're bold, just like your makeup choices. Now quit your griping and hand me that eyelash curler."

A few minutes later, the girls proclaimed me finished.

I went back to the full-length mirror and gaped. I mean, yeah, I know I'm not bad looking, but they'd made me look like someone else entirely. I'd never felt so feminine or attractive in my life. And it felt good. Shania had curled my hair, giving the waves more bounce so that they framed my face perfectly. Somehow, she'd done the same to my eyelashes, without putting a lot of black goop on them. Gold shadow, plum eyeliner and pale pink lipstick made my green eyes pop and pulled the whole look together without looking overdone.

"Wow, Shania. It's like a whole different person." I shook my head, watching the curls sway and bounce in the mirror.

"Pfft, hardly," she scoffed. "It's just a little eyeliner and glitz. We just shined you up a little, is all. Anyone with half an eyeball in their head could see what you look like, makeup or not."

"Well, still, I have to admit. I think I kind of love it."

"In that case, I'll leave you the liner and lipstick. They're a little too cool for my complexion, anyway."

Jules checked her watch, a large modern gold and steel piece that dwarfed her wrist. She'd just gotten it that day, a graduation present from her aunt and uncle. It worked as a timepiece, planner, and Chat unit, complete with a holo keyboard and everything.

"9:30 ladies. Time to go."

Shania threw all her makeup tools back into a bag and we headed down the stairs. I didn't see the boys.

"They must be outside." We went out back, finding Hollis and Khai with my parents and their friends.

"You guys ready to go?" I called, walking up to the group. Everybody turned, watching the three of us approach.

"Um, yeah," Khai said, jumping up. "Hollis, you ready?"

"As ever. Let's go get this party started."

The adults stood, too, saying goodbye.

"Don't you all look lovely," my mom said, lingering as she hugged me.

"I love your makeup," Amber agreed, nodding at Jules, who turned to raise an eyebrow at Shania as if to say, "See?"

My dad leaned back against one of the chairs and looked us over, frowning. Then he turned to the boys. "Don't forget what I said, Hollis. You're driving, you're sober. You keep an eye on your sister and her friends. I know how these parties can get."

"Really, Alec? You hated parties," my mom laughed.

"Exactly," my dad said.

"Don't worry, sir, we'll keep an eye on them," Khai reassured them.

"Me, too, sir. My poppa didn't raise me to drink and drive. Jules hitched a ride with me, but anyone else needs a ride, I'll be available." Shania addressed my dad, but her gaze lingered a little too long on my brother, earning her a glare from both Jules and I. Not that Hollis noticed.

"Alright then, you girls have a good time. You, too, boys." My dad nodded, and my mom rushed over to give us all one more hug.

"I see you're finally wearing those boots I gave you," she whispered happily in my ear. "Do they feel good? They fit?"

"I think so, yeah." I nodded.

And the thing was, I was starting to think maybe they really did.

Chapter 7

An hour in at the party, and I was beginning to rethink my friends' choice of shoes. I wasn't used to heels. It didn't matter if the soles were cushy. My feet were beginning to ache, and my toes felt crowded within the boots' dainty points.

But, I wasn't bored.

Boys had been coming up to me one after the other, saying how they'd miss me, giving me over-friendly hugs. Even more shocking? They actually knew my name. Either someone was feeding them info before they got to me, or I hadn't been as much of a wallflower as I thought. Either way, it didn't matter. Now, tonight, my cover was definitely blown.

I never drank at parties, heck, I never came to parties, but when my feet started really hurting and the sixth guy offered to get me a drink, I figured I might as well. All the couches were taken with couples making out like they'd never see each other again. Maybe they wouldn't. What did I know about love, or romance? Sure, I'd dated a bit in school, but no one had really caught my fancy for long. Nothing that made me want to hang in there for the long haul or initiate the surge.

That was another way we were luckier now than my parents had been. The surge, the intense physical bonding between couples that allowed emotions to transfer between them along an empathic connection was no longer reserved for those lucky enough to find one of their spiritually, physically compatible soul-mates. The Flare had changed fae and humans enough that people could now access that connection at will, harnessing the light within their own bodies to trigger the bonding, and the intense physical sensations that were said to go along with it.

Once you had the surge, it could never be broken. Or maybe it could, but who would want to break it?

Answer: no one.

Divorce rates were at a record low throughout the world, thanks to the surge. Couples like my mom and dad, people who met and had that instant attraction, that immediate knowing that lit the entire body, they still cropped up, too – more common now than they had been thirty years ago. But the naturals were the minority. Anybody could have the surge, if they wanted to. You just needed a willing partner, and an intense tantric moment to wake up the kundalini, or body lightning to activate and synchronize your DNA, and that was it. You were golden. Your fate as a happily-forever-after couple was sealed.

At least, I thought that's how it worked. Like I said, I wouldn't have known, at least not from personal experience.

So yeah. At the party, feeling attractive, I let the attention go to my head. Hollis had been cornered the minute he got there by Suki's older sister, Sienna, who was also back on break and challenged him to a drinking contest she clearly was hoping to lose. So much for being the responsible adults. They'd made a pretty good dent in the bottle, and then progressed to what I could only guess was a game of truth or dare. Mostly, they seemed to be picking dare.

Jules groaned. "Do you see that? Gods, your brother is such a-"

"I know, trust me," I said, rolling my eyes.

A song came on, something full of pop and pep, and Shania squealed.

"Come on, girls, let's dance!"

I thought about the floor, and my feet. I saw guy number six, Tim, coming back with two drinks and I shook my head.

"Nah, I'm going to sit this one out." I hopped up on a newly vacated stool and waved them away. Ah. Divine relief.

Shania shrugged, dragging Jules away to disappear among the dancers in the cleared-out dining room. Tim, an A-list techie I'd had maybe one class with ever, approached with a grin.

"Here you go, one beer special, hand delivered."

"Why, thank you, Tim," I bowed my head, taking the cup from him with a flourish and taking a swig. I looked into the cup, swirling it gently as I tried to decipher its pale blue tint. "Not bad. What kind of beer is this?"

"Whatever cheap stuff Carl brought," he said, taking a healthy sip of his own. Carl was another Techie, and one of our star Lacrosse players.

"So what makes it so special? Aside of course, from it being hand delivered." I smiled. My gods, was I flirting? I took another sip. Yep. I thought I was.

"A couple shots of Roumkivara 'shine." He winked, and I knew I was in trouble. Roumkivara moonshine was distilled from Cala, the Aeden grass that had special healing and energizing properties. Brewed with the silver waters of Valhalla, the spirit was said to have curative properties. It also only took a few shots of it to render most grown men giddy with joy.

Still, it's not like it was illegal or anything. The drinking age had been lowered years ago to coincide with the age of Ascension: eighteen. I'd made it through high school without any causing any trouble. Surely one or two cups couldn't hurt anything now?

I looked around to see if someone might stop me from misbehaving, but everyone was out of sight or busy. Even Khai, who had been nearby talking to some guys for the last hour, had walked outside a while ago and he hadn't come back.

I frowned, wondering where he was.

"Everything okay?" Tim asked.

"What? Oh, yeah. Yes." I returned my attention to Tim and smiled. Sitting on the tall stool, we were almost at eye level – another thing I wasn't used to. "Bottoms up!"

I put the cup to my lips and tipped my head back, finishing the smooth, strong beer. I handed the cup back to Tim, who had a huge grin plastered across his face now. "Another?"

"Sure thing, Ana. Here, you take mine, and I'll go get myself another one."

"Okay, great. Thanks!"

Tim weaved back out through the crowd, only to be replaced by Slice, a friend of mine from art class. We called him that, because he had a really unique collage talent and was a wiz with laser knives. Plus, he just looked edgy, the way some people did, you know?

"Hey, Ana, what's up?"

"Oh, you know, same ole, same ole. Graduation, drinking, world domination."

He laughed. "In that order?"

"Pretty much, yeah," I said, smiling up at him. I'd kind of had a thing for Slice in twelfth grade, but it hadn't worked out. Not for me anyway. If memory served, he'd started dating Suki, and I'd lost interest. He hadn't gotten any less cute over the last two years, though.

He must have seen some of that former interest in my eyes, because he watched me finish my second cup of blue beer, took the cup away from and placed it on the bar behind me, and came in close, pressing himself between my knees.

"You know, Ana, I've always thought you were pretty special."

"You did? I mean, you have?"

"I do." He tucked a strand of hair behind my ear.

"That's funny. I used to like you but then you started dating Suki, so-" I clapped a hand over my mouth. "Ooops. I think that 'shine is getting to my head. Forget I said that."

"Why would I? How could I? Ana, I told you, I...Well, let me just show you."

His mouth came down on mine, without invitation or warning, and I squeaked in surprise. Then, my arms wrapped around him and I leaned forward, melting into the heady sensation of being kissed by a former high school crush. Who cared if it wasn't a current crush?

This felt good.

This felt better than good. I found myself questioning my years of self-imposed introversion. If this was what I'd been missing, I might have begged my friends for a makeover years ago.

Better than being nice, than being passed over. This was-

Chapter 8

Suddenly, Slice pulled out of my arms, making me stumble forward off my stool, just barely managing to catch myself so I didn't fall to my knees. I looked around, and saw Slice hadn't been so lucky. Sprawled out on the floor, he seemed to be unconscious.

Was it the 'shine? Poor Slice, I thought, giggling. I started to kneel, wanting to make sure he was okay, when an arm grabbed mine and steered me roughly in the other direction.

"Hey!" I protested, looking up. Khai's face was stormy, his normally blue eyes literally popping with flashes of silver light. He looked so serious. Too serious. Another laugh escaped me, and I tried to look concerned. Something had set off his elemental power, which wasn't easy.

"Wow, Khai, are you alright? You look-"

"I'm taking you home," he ground out. His hand still on my arm, we exited the house and made oour way towards the car. I practically had to run to keep up with his long strides.

"What? Why? Has something happened? Slow down, you're walking too fast." He didn't answer me and I pulled away from him.

"Just get in the damn car, Ana," he said, opening the door.

"You know, you're kind of being an ass," I said smugly, getting in and waiting for the seat harness to secure me safely before turning to watch him climb in the driver's side. "Where's Hollis? You didn't even let me say goodbye to Jules and Shania. We can't just-"

"Hollis is fine. I'll come back for him later." Khai threw the car into gear and we started down the road. "What the hell was that Ana? Drinking 'shine? Making out with some random guy?"

I smiled, leaning back. Khai was taking the curves pretty fast, and my head was spinning.

"That was pretty great, wasn't it? Remember when I had that huge crush on Slice in twelfth grade? He's so cute. A really great artist, too. You know, maybe we should go back and make sure he's okay. I think he passed out." I snickered. "Maybe my kiss was too intense for him. Whaddya think?"

I opened my eyes to look at Khai, and saw sparks coming out of his eyes. Literal. Sparks.

"Um, Khai?"

"We're not going back. Slice is fine, I'm sure of it. Which is more than he deserves, taking advantage of you while you've been drinking."

"Don't be such a fusspot," I teased. "Slice was just being friendly. It was only a little kiss. Gods, I haven't had a good kiss in years," I sighed, closing my eyes. "I should have gone to more parties."

Khai mumbled something I could quite catch.

"What?"

"Nothing. Never mind."

I peeked at him, and saw the light in his eyes start to fade. I closed mine again and settled back, trying to ignore the spinning in my head.

I must have dozed off, because it seemed like moments later that Khai was opening my door and helping me out of the car.

The night air had cooled quite a bit, and my head was feeling clearer. I smiled up at Khai, still feeling rather good from the 'shine and my kiss. Then I remembered something was wrong, something he still hadn't told me about.

"Khai, you still haven't told me, why are we here? What was the big emergency?"

He ran a hand over his neck and swore. "Gods, Ana, how can you be so smart, and so dense at the same time?"

"Hey-"

"I brought you home because you were clearly drunk and letting some guy manhandle you."

"What? I was not!"

"Oh, come on. You know he doesn't care about you. You've never been Slice's type."

That stung.

"What's that supposed to mean?"

"Tarted up, party girls," he said, waving a hand over me, as if somehow I fit that description tonight.

"Seriously? I can't dress up? I can't talk to a few guys? At a party? You're a jerk, Khai. It's not up to you who I talk to, or what I do. It's not up to anyone, but me. He liked me. It felt good. What do you care? It's not like he's my first kiss – you should know, since that happened when you and Hollis let me play spin the bottle with your friends after I threatened to tell Mom and Dad. I don't remember you making a big fuss about protecting my honor when we kissed. What makes you think you can order me around, now?"

Angry, I poked him in the chest, warming up to the topic, stabbing him in time with my next words. "You don't get to tell me what to do." I took a step back, huffing a piece of hair out my face. "You better remember that, or you can just stay home this summer on your own. I don't need you looking over my shoulder all the time."

"Kind of hard not to," he said, smirking down at me.

The reference to my height was the last straw. Irate, I dropped to the ground and struck out with my leg, swiping him off his feet.

I stood up and dusted myself off.

"Who are you?" he asked, looking up at me in surprise. It wasn't often that I was able to get the drop on Khai, or, well, anyone.

Then again, it wasn't often that I was so mad.

"Someone you better start respecting," I said, wagging my finger at him. "Don't forget to pick up Hollis. I think he's making out with Sienna. He could probably use some rescuing, too."

Without waiting to hear an answer, too annoyed to even look at him anymore, I turned and marched towards the house.

Chapter 9

The next morning I woke up feeling refreshed and relaxed. Then, I remembered everything that had happened the night before. A blush crept up my cheeks. Had I really made out with Slice? And knocked Khai off his feet? Oh wow. I'd had a couple sips of Roumkivara moonshine before from my parents' cups, but never drank it freely. Never realized just how strong it could be, or how much it could change a person's behavior. I hoped my friends hadn't been too worried when I'd disappeared from the party.

Still. I couldn't find it in me to regret anything that I'd said, or done. I wasn't lying when I said I hadn't had a great kiss in years. And, as strange as it had felt, it had been nice to feel attractive. Wanted by so many guys.

Speaking of – I realized I was still in the pink sweater from the night before. I vaguely recalled stripping off my skirt and boots and crawling into bed to crash, my head still spinning. I hadn't even said hello to my parents who had still been out back with their friends, my dad playing guitar quietly into the night. I wondered if Khai had talked to them before he left, and what he'd told Hollis when he got back to the party.

I picked up my Chat and called up the holo screen. Eight messages. The first three were from Jules.

"Hey girl, where are you?"

"Ana, you still here? I can't find you or Khai anywhere, and that skank of a brother of yours is still in the corner with Sienna all over him."

"Ana? Call me. I just ran into Slice and he says you guys were making out and then Khai tased him or something?"

That last one made me pause. Not once had Khai indicated that he had assaulted Slice. I'd assumed my would-be suiter had passed out. But if Khai had used his new lightning skills on him... Oh, he was going to be in so much trouble when I told his mom.

I listened to the rest of my messages. A couple from Shania, sounding a lot like Jules. Two from Khai. Apologizing in the first one. Then taking it back and not apologizing in the second. Cave man. The last message was from Jules again.

"Hey girl, it's Jules. I just talked to Khai and he told me what happened. Good for you. It's about time you started standing up for yourself. Anyways, glad you're home safe. It's raining like crazy here and Shania wants to go home before her road washes out. Don't forget we're going shopping tomorrow, I'll pick you up at eleven. Later!"

I looked at my clock and groaned. It was already half past ten. I dragged myself out of bed and threw a robe on, heading for the shower. Ten minutes later I was fresh and dressed, back in some of my favorite attire, leggings and a thigh-skimming lightweight tunic. I looked at the suede boots from the night before and sighed. They *had* been comfortable. After today, I'd be wearing hiking boots and shorts for at least a few weeks.

Why not?

I put on the boots and a pair of dangling crystal earrings, grabbed my purse and went down the stairs, my boots clomping loudly on the wooden treads.

49

"Good morning!" I called out, walking through the house. My mom was in the kitchen cleaning up.

"Hey sweetie. Did you have fun at the party? I didn't hear you guys come in last night. Did you get home before the rain?"

"Me? Oh, yeah. It was okay," I hedged.

She looked at me closely. "Yeah? Anything you want to tell me?"

"No," I huffed.

She made a mocking sound. "You know I can tell when you're lying, right?" She cocked her head and laughed. "Don't sweat it, A. I'm just glad you had a good time. Just don't ever do anything I wouldn't do, okay?"

"Is there such a thing?" I asked.

"Such a thing as what?" My dad said, coming in the room.

"That mom wouldn't do," I supplied.

Dad snorted. "Well, she's never been one for listening to me, that's for sure."

She swatted him with a towel, laughing. "I listen."

"Don't believe her," he said. "She lies."

"Oh, why you-" In a flash, she had wheeled around him in a graceful spin to pin his arms behind him. "Take it back."

"Never." He ducked and flipped her over his shoulder, moving slightly so that instead of landing on the floor, she wound up in his arms. And then, they were kissing.

Ugh. See what I had to put up with?

Parents can be *so* gross.

I turned my back on them, humming to block out the smooching noises, and poured myself a fresh smoothie.

"Hey, I was going to drink that," my mom protested, having come up for air.

"Too late. Consider it payment for traumatizing my young, tender eyes so early in the morning." I knocked back the purple concoction and drank a large portion of it down. "Mmm. Thanks, Mom. Carrots and purple cabbage?"

"No, fresh cala and berries," she said as I took another sip.

I made a face, remembering the night before. The cala-derived shine, the fight with Khai. "You know what? You finish it. I think I'll just have some tea and toast."

"Okay," she said, looking at me strangely. She took the clay cup back from me and sniffed. "It doesn't taste bad, does it? Ewan brought the cala for me special from Valhalla, but if it's not fresh enough-"

"No, no, it's okay. I had enough. You finish it. You made it, after all."

"Suit yourself," my mom said, and grabbed my dad's hand. "Come on, Alec, let's change and go for a run."

I put two slices of oat bread in the toaster, pulled out a jar of fresh honey and set the kettle on the stove to boil. I reached for a cup, and reconsidered. Jules would be here any minute. I switched off the stove and went for some cold sweet tea out of the fridge instead, filling up the large ceramic cup to the brim. Like her own mother, my mom had a taste for eclectic pottery. Frederika had a multi-colored collection of Fiesta-ware that antique dealers lusted after. My mom liked things slightly less colorful, snatching up handmade glazed pottery whenever she saw it. She had over a hundred pieces in varied, dripping shades of plum, teal, and green set against backgrounds of smoke and wood tones. Somehow, it all went together beautifully to create a full kitchen set, big enough to feed our entire extended family of misfits and friends.

My bread had barely popped out of the toaster when Jules walked in. We'd been friends for so long, we were well past the niceties of knocking.

"Ooh, yum!" She grabbed one of the pieces of bread and honey and stuffed half of it in her mouth. "Thanks, Ana," she mumbled in garbled tones so it sounded more like "Spangsabba."

"Want some tea to go with that?" I asked drily.

"Mmm, no thanks." She wiped her mouth. "I'm good. You ready to go?"

"Sure, just let me clean up."

I washed out my cup and wiped down the counter.

"Okay, ready."

"Where's Hollis? Does he need anything at the store? Maybe he wants to come with us?" Jules asked hopefully.

"He's still sleeping. Besides, I'm pretty sure he's all set." I couldn't imagine Captain Wonderful being anything other than one-hundred percent prepared.

"Okay. Khai, too?"

"Khai? He can sleep in a sack and eat pine needles for all I care." I started towards her car.

"Oooh, somebody's cranky today. You know, Khai was pretty cranky last night, too. What exactly happened between you two?" she asked, rushing after me.

"I thought he told you last night." I opened the door to her Chevord solar cruiser and sat down.

She got in the driver's seat and waited for the car to strap her in. "Well, yeah, but you know how guys are. Details, Ana. A girl needs details."

I sighed, telling her everything that had happened. If I didn't do it now, gods knew how she'd pester me on the trip, and then Hollis and Khai would get in on the conversation, too.

"Oh. My. Gods. So Khai really did tase Slice? He told me he just pulled the guy off of you. Wayne found Slice passed out on the floor and carried him upstairs to sleep it off. What a total jerk! Talk about double standards. I didn't see Khai rescuing Hollis at any point," she said bitterly. "Even when Sierra's tongue was all the way-"

"Ugh, please, spare me the details." I held a hand up to ward off her words. "I agree. They are both jerks. No, I take that back. They are all jerks. Slice, Tom, Khai, Hollis. All of them."

Jules nodded. "Dudes suck."

"Totally," I agreed.

We drove quietly for a while, and then she pointed at my feet. "So, the boots, huh? Those are different. Does this mean some of our makeover stuck?"

"Maybe," I winked. "They are really comfortable."

"Only you would talk about comfort and those boots in the same sentence, I swear, Ana."

"What? They are."

"I know, but that's not the point. They're hot."

"Whatever," I said, feeling embarrassed. "I just figured I'd get some wear out of them before we hit the trail tomorrow."

She nodded, agreeing with me.

"So..." she started after another pause. "I get why Khai was upset, I mean, he and Hollis are practically your legal guardians, but what about you? Why are you so mad at Khai? Did you actually want to stay at the party?"

She sounded like it was the least likely notion she'd ever heard.

"Actually, yeah," I said, blushing. "You remember, I had that crush on Slice back in twelfth? Gods, I thought he was so hot. Turns out, he's a pretty dreamy kisser, after all."

"Ana, you dog! And here we all assumed Khai was saving you."

"I'm not some hapless damsel in need of saving, you know. I can take of myself."

"I know that," she said, sounding like I was insane to think otherwise. "But Khai's a guy. According to them, we're *all* just dying for them to save us. Just look at Prince Charming. Dude happens across an unconscious female in the woods, and what is the first thing he does? Kisses her. I mean, come on, how creepy is that? Who does that?"

"Yeah, you're right. The Grimms really gave fairy tales a bad name."

"Seriously. Your mom's were so much better. I used to love listening to her tell stories when we were little."

"I know, right? Anyways, what all do we still need on this trip?" I asked, changing the subject.

"Well, I was thinking of getting one of those camp hammocks so I can sleep out under the stars sometimes. And I need more stove fuel. And a better flashlight."

"Good idea, I think I'll get one of those hammocks, too. I need a better water bottle, too. Mine drips sometimes. And one of those personal sonic-tizers."

"Oh, good call! I didn't even think of that. Can we share? I'll split the cost with you. Those things are expensive."

"Sure, no problem." Who was I to deny someone access to a PST? The small handheld devices could do everything a sink at home could do, in an instant. Who needed toilet paper or a sink to wash up? With a PST you could just lick your platters clean and then sanitize them. Easy peasy. They wouldn't handle cleaning all our clothes, but they could spot-clean.

We spent an hour shopping, comparing prices and looking at useless junk we didn't need. We were just finishing up when my Chat pinged. I glanced at the holo screen and frowned.

"What is it?" Jules asked.

"Just Khai."

"Aren't you going to answer it?"

"Not today. Whatever it is, he can wait till tomorrow."

"Wow, are you sure those aren't, like, magic boots?" she asked, grinning.

"Why do you say that?' I said, mystified.

"Because, since you put them on you've been making out, drinking, shopping, and now you're not talking to Khai. I mean, come on, you talk more to Khai on that thing that you talk to me."

"That's not true!"

She raised an eyebrow.

"Okay, fine, maybe it's slightly true. Whatever. The boots aren't magic, I'm just...I'm tired of being protected and coddled all the time. I'm not weak just because I'm small."

"No, but-"

"Don't say it," I said shaking my head. "There are no buts. Not anymore. I don't need anyone to protect me. I'm a grown woman. Got it?"

"Hey, you know I agree. Totally. I'm just saying, don't be so hard on Khai. I'm sure he was just trying to be a good friend."

I glared at her. Had she heard me at all?

She chuckled and threw an arm around my shoulder. "Alright. Don't look at me like that. You know I'm always on your side. Come on. I think some pizza is in order."

Chapter 10

"He said I looked like a tart."

I mumbled the words through a mouthful of Mexican pizza with cheddar cheese, tomatoes and jalapenos.

"Who did?" Jules asked, confused.

"Khai. He said the only reason Slice was paying attention to me was because I looked like a party girl."

"No, he did not!" Jules exclaimed, looking outraged.

"He did." I took a sip of my soda. "And then, he made fun of me being short."

"What?!"

"Well, okay, not in so many words, but I told him he couldn't talk down to me, and he said it'd be hard not to."

"Oh, my God. What did you say?"

"Say? I knocked him on his ass."

"No."

"Yes. I was so mad, I could barely speak."

"Oh wow, those boots really *are* magic." She laughed. "I wish I could have seen his face."

"It was pretty great," I grinned back.

"Still, I can't believe he would disrespect you like that. What an ass. And the boots! You looked great, nothing tarty about it. But you know, you guys are practically like family. Sounds like he was just being over-protective, seeing his cuz' all grown up and getting some adult attention. I'm glad you set him straight."

"Me, too."

"You going to be okay tomorrow? This doesn't affect our trip, does it?"

"Nah. We'll be okay, I guess. I'll get over it. I mean, I know I was acting a little out of character, drinking shine and everything. You're probably right – he probably thought he was doing me a favor. I just don't want to talk to him today, okay?"

"Fine by me. So, what should we do for the rest of the day?"

"I don't know," I mused. "See a movie? I'm definitely all shopped out. I can't stay out too late, either, my mom and dad are taking us out to dinner, and I still have to pack."

"Yeah, that sounds cool. There's a new one I want to see with that Peters guy in it. You know, the one with the moon spirits?"

"Sure, okay." I called up the theatre times on my chat. "It's playing in twenty minutes."

"Perfect. You get lunch, movie's on me?"

"Sounds good." I pulled out my wallet and left a hundred on the table. "Ready?"

"Yep." She picked up the last of her crust in one hand. "Let's jet."

We killed a few hours at the movie theatre, one of the older 3D immersive entertainment centers with holo seats. I hated the newer theatres, the ones where you wore headsets and body suits. Everybody else thought it was cool feeling like you were in the movie, but I thought living was enough reality for me. I wanted to watch the fantasies, not be flooded by them. I liked to enjoy the laughter of my friends, to hear the rest of the audience, not be completely cut off and consumed by the mindplay.

Jules said I was too sensitive, but she didn't mind putting up with the older tech for me. Even though she enjoyed the new theatres, which had starting popping up in our county several years ago, she agreed it was more fun laughing together.

By the time the movie was over, I was feeling completely relaxed and happy. Jules drove me home, promising to meet me at the trail at nine am the following morning.

"Hey Mom, Dad, I'm home!" I called as walked in.

"In the library," my mom yelled back.

"Hey guys," I said, making my way over to the long desk they were sharing, working side by side on their computers. Honestly, they were too cute. I mean, seriously. They never seemed to get tired of each other. Which was good, since they'd probably live another several hundred years. "Whatcha doing?"

"Following up on a new lead. Remember those hieroglyphic carvings we found in the hidden tunnels under Cappadocia the first time we went to Turkey?"

"How could I forget," I said drily. "It's only, like your favorite story."

"Well, it was our honeymoon," my dad grinned, reaching out to hold my mom's hand.

I groaned and bit back a smile.

"Right, well, I think we've found our Rosetta stone, something we can use to decode the writing," my mom said, glowing with excitement.

"What? No way! That's so cool."

"Tell me about it. A colleague of ours has found an inscribed tablet coated in gold. She hasn't figured out what it's made of, yet, but it has writing on it in the oldest form of Sumerian cuneiform that appears to be a translation of the carvings, carefully transcribed and addressed to a ruler named Utu. She was leading some students in a dig at Larsa, in Iraq, and one of them found a room. Apparently, it has quite a few of these gold tablets, but this is the only one with Sumerian accompanying the other text. Elsa thinks it might have been Utu's private office or library."

"Wow. So, when do you get to see it?" I asked.

My mom and dad looked at each other.

"What?"

"Well, that's kind of what we wanted to talk to you guys about at dinner," my mom said. "See, Elsa's staying at Larsa for the rest of the summer. She's procured a huge grant since the find. She's asked us to come and consult on the dig."

"But, that's awesome! Why the long faces?"

"Well, you know, with you kids going on the hike..." My father began, and trailed off.

"So?"

"Well, we just don't like being so far away from the two of you. What if something happens?"

"What if...?" I trailed off and thought. "Look you guys go away all the time and we've made it through somehow.

Here or there, you wouldn't be with us either way. We'll be fine."

"Which is what I've been telling him," my mom agreed, a gleam in her eye. "And he knows it, too. I think somebody's just not quite ready to see their little girl all grown up." She patted his hand and he looked at me, rolling his eyes as he shrugged.

"Guilty as charged," he admitted. "So what do you think? Are you sure you're okay with us being a whole world away this summer?"

"Totally," I laughed, and his face fell a bit. Apparently, he really wasn't ready to let go, yet. My mom made a face at me and I backtracked. "I mean, yeah. We'll be okay, Dad. You've taught us well, and we have those GPS things you got us. Honestly, you have nothing to worry about. I swear. The trails should be crawling with other hikers, anyway. It's not like we'll be alone."

"You're right. I know you're right. Both of you." He sighed and ran a hand along his neck and through his hair, setting it on end. My dad's hair was chronically crazed. My mom said it was one her favorite things about him. "Okay, Ana, how about you round up your brother and we can head out for dinner?"

"Sounds good, Dad." On impulse, I leaned down, gave him a hug and kissed his cheek.

"What was that for?" he asked, leaning back a bit, surprise making his violet eyes glow a little brighter than usual.

"Nothing." I shrugged. "Just, I love you."

"I love you, too, bug," he said, pulling me in for another hug. Over his shoulder, my mom mouthed "thank you" at me, and I blew her a kiss.

I left the room and jogged up the stairs to my room where I threw my bag of new gear on the bed and changed into a fresh shirt. A belt around my waist cinched the embroidered peasant blouse my parents had brought me from one of their trips to create a leaner look. I ran my fingers through my hair, twirling some of the waves back into curls and decided to pin one side back with a small clip. My dad's part human heritage had decided to show itself in my genes with a mild pointing at the tip of each ear. Nothing like what you saw in old movies, but they weren't round, either. Since more humans and fae were hooking up these days, more and more kids had them. Regularly, you couldn't really tell a fae from a human. They all looked the same – although we did tend to be better looking than your average Joe. Good genes, Jade said.

But when you mixed human and fae DNA, sometimes funny things happened. Some kids had webbed toes. Some had eyes that glowed, or came in strange colors, like my father. And some, like me, had pointy ears. My mom thought it was just nature's way of working towards something great. Something better. She always thought the best of everyone, even Mother Nature. Of course, in a way, she was Mother Nature. Or part of it. Without her energy merging with the Tree of Life, humans wouldn't have been shifting closer to fae, and the earth would still be covered in wars and greed and chaos.

Anyway, I liked my ears. I was proud of my dad, and his dual heritage. The first thing I'd done when my mom said I could finally pierce my ears was to get lab-grown emerald studs put in at the tips. I still wore them every day.

Something else I'd gotten from my dad's side of the family? His mom's very human, very tiny stature. That, I wasn't quite as proud of, but there wasn't much I could do about it.

I glossed my lips with Shania's pink shimmer and decided I was ready to go. As much fun as dressing up the night before had been, the fact was that I was a simple kind of a girl. A little bit of sparkle and shine, some comfortable clothes that didn't make me look too small or round, and I was done. Of course, I wasn't quite ready to give up the buttery suede boots, not yet. Tomorrow would be soon enough.

I walked through my bathroom and into Hollis' room, knocking as I opened the door.

"Hey brother, time to hit the road. You ready?"

"Yeah, just a sec." He finished typing something into his computer and shut it down. "Ready."

"Cool. Mom and Dad are waiting downstairs." I led the way out and Hollis followed.

"So, I hear you had a pretty fun time last night. Made quite an impression on that guy, Slice. He was asking for you, after you left."

"Yeah, well. Apparently Khai thought I was having a little too much fun," I grumbled.

He snickered. "Yeah, I gathered that. He read me the riot act for not paying more attention to you. Like you need my protection."

"I know, right? What the heck are you guys learning at school, anyways, that he's turning into such a tight-ass?"

"I don't know. We're not in all the same classes."

"Clearly. I mean, really, Sienna? Again?"

"Hey, she's a great girl."

"I know, but you guys never last."

"So? I'm not looking for anything that will last. Not yet. I'm not ready for anything like that."

"I know. She just seems..."

"What?"

"I don't know. She's nice enough. I just think you could find someone you have more in common with, don't you?"

"Dangerous thoughts, Ana-banana. If we have too much in common, I might start thinking I want to stick around. You know?"

"Would that be so bad?"

"Would what be so bad?" my mom asked, coming into the hall, followed by my dad.

"Nothing," Hollis and I answered at the same time. I knew the last thing he wanted was to discuss his love-life with Mom. If the truth came out, he'd probably throw me under the bus and tell her what had happened with Slice.

"Okay then," she said, eyeing us both like we'd stolen cookies from a jar. Neither of us said a word. "Well, let's go then, reservation's in twenty minutes."

"Great," said my dad, grabbing his keys. "Hollis, maybe you can go over your route one more time with me while we drive."

I groaned.

"Again?" asked Hollis.

"Again," confirmed my dad.

"Dad," I said, teasing. "You do realize we might change our mind while we walk, explore some other routes? Who knows what hidden gems other hikers might tell us about."

"Of course, I realize. But this way, when you make a deviation, I'll know where and when."

"Humor your father, dear," my mom said, patting Hollis' arm. "Maybe this way we can actually eat in peace."

"Fat chance," I muttered. I knew Dad would have us going over the route a few more times, between quizzing us on what to do in different emergency situations. I was already anticipating the reward of a very large, very gooey chocolate lava cake to ease the pain.

For someone who lived life searching for the undiscovered in uncharted places, he sure hated surprises.

Chapter 11

"So remember, if a thunderstorm comes up what do you do?"

"Hide behind Hollis?" I joked.

"No, Ana," my dad said, all seriousness. "Lightning can hit you in three ways, through the ground, a side-flash or direct cloud-to-ground. All three are dangerous. You'll need to-"

"Get away from tall trees and high ground, and squat on top of my pack or a big rock on top of other boulders without putting my hands on the ground. Got it, Dad. I remember."

"We're gonna be fine, Dad," Hollis said, throwing an arm around each of us. "It's not like this is our first camping trip. And Ana's right. I can help us get grounded if I need to. I've been practicing."

"Yeah, Alec, and I can help him practice more, too." Khai cackled, waggling his fingers at us all.

"Please, Khai, be careful out there. The last thing anyone needs is a forest fire started by irresponsible faelings."

"Not faelings, Dad," I reminded him, grinding my teeth. "We're all over eighteen."

"Right. No. Of course you are. Sorry, bug," he said, ruffling my hair. "Old habits die hard."

We were standing at the nearest trailhead for the Long Trail, waiting for Jules to show up. So far, I hadn't killed Khai, deciding to maintain a distant air of civility and pretend that part of me wasn't still seething at his interference two days before. At some point, I knew, we'd have to talk it out. And no one could ever stay mad at Khai for long. At present, though, the best idea seemed to be keeping my distance.

Waiting in the parking lot over the state border in Massachusetts, this tactic was starting wear thin. I couldn't wait for Jules to arrive so we could start walking. Plus, she'd make a great buffer between me and the boys.

The Long Trail officially starts at the Mass/Vermont border – and the only way to get to there is to hike in. We'd had a couple options of trails to start on, and had decided to go with the most well-known, an Appalachian Trail section that climbs the steep slope of East Mountain through the Clarksburg State Forest. The AT actually follows the Long Trail for just over 100 miles, so we'd be sharing the woods with a lot of hikers at the beginning, since the AT is so well-traveled. The further north we got, the quieter the trail would become. At least, that's what my End-to-End Guide said.

My dad insisted he would wait with us until Jules got there and we hiked off into the wilds. He blamed my mom, saying she wanted a picture of us all at the start before we left. We knew better, of course. It was just Dad, being Dad.

And yes. He was still giving us instructions on how to survive.

Fashionably late as usual, Jules finally arrived. My dad spent some time reassuring Mrs. Harrison that the wise, older boys would take care of us young girls (you can imagine the faces Jules and I were making at this point) and even went so far as to make Hollis and I show off our new GPS watches. Then, it was time to go.

We'd all made a pact weeks ago not to use our Chats on the trip, not even for photo posting, so we could really "go wild" and experience the isolation of the trail. Now, we dropped the earpieces into a tiny, waterproof box. Jules locked it, looping the key's lanyard around her neck and tucking it into her shirt, and handed the box to Hollis for safekeeping. Khai'd been designated trail photographer, so he was allowed use of a holo-cam, a small device that easily fit in any pocket and would upload the photos to each of our cloud servers via satellite; we wouldn't be able to see them, though, until we left the trail. I was the record keeper, and had a small journal in my pack for detailing the highs and lows of our journey.

We hugged our parents, posed for their obligatory holo-vids and walked silently into the cool, damp green of the summer wood.

The air was cool, the sun still low in the morning sky, and almost immediately my boots began to collect dew as we tromped through the previous season's litter of leaves upon the ground. Luckily, these hiking boots were heavily waterproofed and well-worn. Anticipating at least a few days of wet weather, I had packed rain pants and gaiters, too. Wet feet on a hike could spell all sorts of trouble, creating unwanted friction and fostering foot-rot. I knew enough to avoid both. We'd traveled much of the AT portion of the Long Trail with my parents growing up, going on day hikes and long-weekend trips whenever the weather and our schedules permitted. As teens, we'd all done plenty of weekend trips with friends, too. We were ready for this.

As if confirming my thoughts, a hawk's cry echoed through the forest. I couldn't understand what it said, not the way my mother would have been able to, but I felt its spirit, the whisper of a greeting sent straight to my soul.

We walked quietly, no one talking, following the painted blazes on the trees towards our destination, the start of the Long Trail. I think each of us was busy contemplating what we wanted out of this hike, where it would take us.

Not just north.

No. Somewhere, more.

Long treks like this were said to bring the walkers more deeply into themselves, highlighting what was truly important, and what was not. I hoped that after the walk we would all be closer friends. I hoped that I would be more me, stronger, better. I wasn't sure exactly what that would be, but still, I hoped for it.

I imagined that the others pondered the same things, but I could be wrong. Knowing Hollis, he wasn't thinking at all. He'd always been good at shutting off his internal dialogue, it was part of why he was such a great instinctual fighter. Or so my dad often said, encouraging me to do the same.

Please.

As if my mind could ever turn off.

Even now, even on the trail, my mind was going along at a good clip. So much so, I barely registered the day hikers that ambled by from time to time with their dogs, and I didn't notice Khai drop back from his place in front with Hollis to walk beside me until his voice cut through my thoughts.

"Hey."

"Hey," I said, keeping my voice neutral.

"You didn't take my calls."

I shrugged. "I didn't want to talk to you."

"I wasn't sure you'd be here today," he said, flatly.

I looked at him, surprised. "Really? How much of a drama queen do you think I am? We've been planning this for months."

"I know, but... I wasn't sure how mad you were. That was a pretty great leg sweep, by the way."

"Yeah, I guess I fight better when I'm pissed." I grinned, looking at him for the first time. He grinned back, his eyes lighting up.

"Guess we've found your super power."

"Rage?"

His face fell a little bit, but the ghost of a smile remained. "I was going to say emotion, but yeah, that'll do."

I laughed. "Don't be so down, Khai. Jules pointed out you probably thought you were doing me a favor, saving me from Slice. Just, next time, maybe ask me if I need help first?"

"Deal." He paused. "Listen, I'm sorry about the other things I said, too. Making fun of your height, that was a low blow." I raised an eyebrow at him and he threw his hands up in front of himself protectively. "No pun intended, I swear. You looked great, really."

"I know, I totally did, right? But thanks, apology accepted."

Khai exhaled, a heavy sigh of relief.

"Thank the gods. I wasn't sure what scared me more, that you might skip the trip because of something stupid I said, or that you'd come along but never talk to me again."

"Bah. You know me. I can't hold a grudge to save my life."

"I don't know. You've surprised me several times already this week. Now? I'm ready for anything."

"Duly noted. I'll try and think of something good."

"Perfect."

We walked on in companionable silence for a while. Ahead, Jules looked over her shoulder and smiled at me, clearly happy that we seemed to have worked things out. Then, she picked up her pace to join Hollis further ahead and match his stride.

"You think Hollis has any idea what he's in for on this trip?" Khai asked wryly.

"I doubt it. He hasn't caught on yet," I said, thinking of the numerous times Jules had thrown herself at him over the last several years. "He talks to you more about stuff like that more than he does to me. He really has no idea she likes him?"

"Not that he's mentioned. I think he's got her firmly relegated to the little sister category."

I looked at Jules, her minuscule tan shorts showing off incredibly fit, gleaming ebony legs a mile long. I knew she'd picked them out less for practicality, and more for a certain man's benefit.

"We'll see. If I know Jules, she's mapped out an epic plan of attack."

"I don't doubt it. Shall we make a wager? I say, Hollis won't notice her at all, and even if he does it will end with tears by the time we reach Mad River," he said, referring to one of the many ski resorts the trail would cut through.

I hated the offhand way he was dismissing Jules. Irritated, the same feelings I'd had after the party bubbled through me.

"Fine. You're on. My money's on Jules."

"Seriously?" he laughed.

"Seriously," I said, glaring at him. "You're underestimating the power of the Jules."

"Okay." I could see his mind churning as he thought it over. A light drizzle started, falling from a small cloud passing overhead, and I pulled off my sunglasses, hooking them in the neck of my shirt.

"Deal," he said finally. "What are we betting? First shower rights when we hit civilization?"

"Boring," I drawled. "I think winner should get ruling rights over the loser for one whole day."

"Ruling rights?" We hadn't gambled for ruling rights since we were kids. Whoever won would be able to order the other person around for the whole day, like a queen with a servant. "Feeling a little confidant, are we?"

I shrugged. "If you think Jules can't do it, what are you worried about?"

"Oh, I'm not worried. Ruling rights it is. Winner to be determined at Mad River?"

"Sounds good to me." We stopped, and shook hands.

"And no cheating. Jules and Hollis can't know," he said, narrowing his eyes at me.

"Of course not!" I said, pretending mock outrage.

"Okay, then, you're on."

Chapter 12

By local standards, it was a steep climb to the start of the Long Trail. Since the Long Trail begins at the state border and follows the ridges of the Green Mountains through Vermont, the only way to get there is up. Both the AT and the Long Trail were known by hikers as the "green tunnel." The name was apt. If you were hiking mid-summer, you were surrounded by dense green foliage, above, to the right, on your left. Sky views were scarce, scenic lookouts a rare treat.

I loved it. I'd grown up in a family of earth fae, and the forest was my home, powers or not. The wilderness had never been something to fear, but a place of comfort and release. My only regret was that Ayita hadn't been able to accompany us. The Long Trail was not horse friendly, and while I was sure Ayita could handle just about any terrain under the sun, horses weren't allowed most of the way. Rather than try and argue the difference between a fleet and a horse to the Green Mountain Club, I'd left her behind.

Now, I stood before a large, wood-burned sign. It read:

"Welcome to the Long Trail, a Footpath in the Wilderness. The Long Trail, maintained by the Green Mountain Club, follows the Green Mountain Range for 273 miles north to Canada. White painted blazes mark

the trail. Blue blazes mark side trails. The A.T. follows the L.T. for 105 miles."

I'd just caught up with the rest of the group. Jules was bouncing around excitedly, ready to go; Hollis was reading the sign and Khai was taking a picture of him.

"Hey look, guys, I'm in two places at once," Jules hooted and straddled the state line, spreading her legs into a near split. Khai laughed and snapped off a couple shots of her posing there as she shifted into a lengthy back bend. A couple of older guys were walking by, heading south, and I asked them to get a shot of the four of us by the sign. Jules resumed her initial pose.

"You guys hiking through the AT?" the guy taking the picture asked.

"Long Trail," Hollis answered.

"Cool. We're hoping to do that next summer. Just day-tripping for now."

"Nice."

"All set," the guy said. "Here you go, Legs." He tossed the camera to Jules and winked. "Happy trails."

"Thanks, you, too," Jules said, passing the camera back to Khai and standing up straight.

The men turned and started walking down the trail, and we did the same, heading north.

"Hey, Legs, wait up!" I laughed, jogging to catch up with Jules.

"Legs, really?"

"You answered to it. You're stuck with it."

"Huh?"

"Oh my gods, have you not heard of trail names?"

"What are you talking about?" she asked, exasperated.

"Trail names. They're nicknames for people doing the whole trail. Everybody thru-hiking gets one eventually. If you respond when someone uses it, that's it, it sticks."

"And mine is Legs?"

"Could be worse," I shrugged. "I've heard some pretty terrible ones. Gold Digger for the guy who dug up someone else's pit toilet by accident. Vulture Chow for the guy who would stalk other people while they were eating, snatching up anything they didn't want. Oh, and there was this girl, named Dumpster Monkey, you don't even want to know why."

Jules mock shivered. "Gah. I'll stick with Legs. What about you? Should we make one up now?"

"Nah. It's gotta be earned. You know, there's gotta be a story behind it. I can wait."

"Oka-ay. Well, I promise if someone tries to give you a crap name I'll gag you so you can't answer to it."

"Awesome, then I'll be known as Gaggy or something."

She cackled. "Yeah, Gabby Gaggy! Oh, oh, or, Silent Protest!"

"Oh. My. Gods. You are so not allowed to give me a nickname."

"What's this," Hollis asked, the boys coming up behind us.

"Nothing, we were just talking about Jules' new trail name," I said, not wanting to give Hollis any ideas.

"She got a trail name?" Khai asked. "Already?"

"Yeah, where were you? Those guys back there – they named her Legs."

"Legs, huh?" Hollis said, taking a long look up and down Jules body. A slow grin came over his face as his eyes traveled over her legs a second time in a way they never had before. "It fits."

I looked at Khai, raising my eyebrows with a smirk. I was so going to win this bet. Thank you, random strangers.

Chapter 13

The weather was promising to be gorgeous the first night, so Jules and I were setting up our camp hammocks while Khai and Hollis worked on making a fire ring. We'd taken it relatively easy today, following the Long Trail up and down several hills for about eight miles before blazing our own path through the woods towards Lake Hancock a few hours before sunset. We'd heard it could be a nice place to camp privately and swim, if you knew where you were going. Thanks to some friends of my dad's, we did. I wasn't entirely sure about the swimming part though – locals also called it Sucker Pond, since certain parts of the water hosted more than their fair share of leeches. The small beach we'd set up next to wasn't supposed to be one of them – I planned on letting Hollis prove that theory.

I looked over at my brother now. Khai had just finished placing the last rock in the ring, and Hollis was using his powers to meld the rocks together as one, creating an impenetrable fire barrier. His affinity with rocks was something he'd inherited from our grandfather, Bran, allowing him to move and shape them in mind-bending ways. I chewed my lip, watching him with envy. I would have been so happy just to make a seed sprout.

I shook my head, dismissing the thought, and put some weight on the hammock, checking that it was secured.

It held.

Since it wasn't raining, I decided to throw up my ground tarp as a screen off to one side, making a private changing area. Normally, I'd just change in my sleeping bag – a skill I'd mastered at a young age – but this was so much more civilized. Satisfied, I grabbed some things out of my pack and headed behind the screen. A minute later, I emerged in a sporty two-piece bathing suit, green with pink polka dots.

"Oh, great idea, Ana," Jules said, digging into her own pack to find her suit and change.

"Girls," my brother said, watching Jules disappear behind the curtain. He stood up, dusted off his hands and quickly stripped down to his underwear. "Race ya!" He grinned at me and turned, running towards the water.

Knowing I'd never catch him, I still gave chase. It's what sisters do, right? "Come on, Khai," I shouted as I passed. "Last one in's a rotten egg!"

He laughed, dropped the load of dead wood he'd been carrying, just missing his bare feet, and pulled his shirt over his head.

"Rotten egg?" Hollis yelled from the water. "Screw that. Loser cooks dinner!"

In moments, Khai was on my tail. "Not me," he laughed, catching up quickly.

"Dudes, that is so not fair!" Jules hollered, sprinting towards us, still tying her bikini behind her neck. Unlike me, she'd opted for something a lot more eye-catching, four tiny gold triangles that just barely covered anything. At least she'd found a way to keep her pack weight down.

Despite her best efforts, Jules was last, Khai and I crashing into the clear, calm water simultaneously and diving under before she had come close to approaching the lake's edge.

"You lose!" Hollis crowed at Jules jogged into the water.

In response, she drew back an arm and aimed a crest of water straight at his face. "Hope you like rock soup," she teased.

Hollis shook the water out of his hair and narrowed his eyes at her. "Oh. You are dead." He disappeared under the water. Moments later, so did Jules. I grinned at Khai.

"Now who's the loser?" I asked.

Jules came up, sputtering, barely catching her breath before Hollis burst out of the water like Poseidon, caught her up in his arms, and crashed back beneath the surface again.

"Don't count your eggs before they hatch, Alvarsson."

"Oh, don't worry, these eggs are golden." I giggled, pointing at the all-out splash war ensuing behind me.

"You wish," he laughed, sounding unworried, and broke into a crawl, making his way out towards the middle of the lake.

I fell back into the water, content to float and stare up at the sky. Clear blue, dotted with small, fluffy dots of white. A rabbit chasing a squirrel. A wine glass that slowly morphed into a spade. Feeling supremely relaxed, I watched the shapes emerge in the clouds. A dragon. An angel. A firetruck.

Someone walked by me, droplets of water splashing my face, and I looked up. Hollis and Jules were returning to shore, chatting and laughing as they went.

I went back to floating.

Why interrupt a good thing?

Swimming had always been one of my favorite pastimes. Just being near the water, whether sea or pond, had a way of smoothing my nerves, erasing worries from my mind.

By the time I tried to stand, I'd strayed a couple hundred feet out from shore to where the water was well above my head. I ducked below the surface, slicking back my hair, and headed for camp. I kept my kicks shallow, the dense weeds below creeping me out each time they brushed against my legs. Even though I knew they were just plants, I couldn't quite shake an old, irrational fear of sea monsters lurking below. When I was eight, I'd wandered into a patch of seaweed underwater at our favorite lake and been convinced an octopus was trying to grab me in the inky blackness. Despite knowing what had really happened, the childhood memory remained strong enough to make me keep my legs well out of any frond's reach.

Once I was back in the clear area we'd started from, I stood, my toes squishing in the soft silt below. I walked out of the water and wiped some of the droplets from my skin with the edge of my hand. Towels were a trail luxury that hadn't made the cut.

I sat down on a large flat rock Hollis had raised near the fire circle, one of four convenient seats. No fire had been started yet, but the stone was warm from the sun.

"So, Jules, what's for dinner?" I asked lazily, glancing over my shoulder to where she had just emerged, dressed for the evening in lightweight pants and a tee shirt.

"Hmm, let's see... I have peas and rice, barley and corn surprise, curried beans with tomatoes, and a kale-kasha combo. All dehydrated, of course."

"Corn surprise? Intriguing," Hollis said, not looking up from the engineering book he was reading. Even considering the near-weightlessness of modern paper, his off-theme choice in trail reading material confounded me. I'd packed a hilarious old memoir about the AT called "A Bear in the Woods," and a compilation of works by Thoreau.

"Okay, corn surprise it is," Jules said, lighting up. She bounced over to the tree where we had hung our supplies out of the reach of bears, and pulled down what she needed. I decided to help her, pulling on a tee shirt over my suit and collecting water from the lake in the collapsible jug we'd brought. I added a drop of silver water from Valhalla, waited the required three minutes for purification, and took a sip. Perfect.

I handed it to Jules, who set to rehydrating the food. Then, she began fiddling with the fire, experimenting with the flint starter kit she'd picked up. A couple sparks flew into the air towards the tinder, but nothing fire worthy.

"This thing sucks," she complained.

"Well, at least we'll have plenty of time to perfect our technique," I laughed. "I'll go get a lighter, hang on."

"Need some help?" Khai called, emerging from the water behind Jules. I looked up, noting new muscles rippling along my friend's chest that I didn't remember from the year before. Always rather gangly when he was younger, I guessed Khai was finally beginning to fill out. I wondered if the girls at McGill chased him now the way they chased my brother. If they did, he'd never mentioned it.

"Yeah, thanks, Khai," Jules said, rocking back on her heels. "I can't figure this thing out."

"No worries, just give me a sec." He made his way over to us, dripping all over Jules, and reached out a hand towards the pit, aiming a small arc of lightning towards the pile of dry moss and leaves under the wood Jules had stacked. Immediately, it smoldered, and then burst into flame.

"Nice one, Sparky," I said. "Glad to see you can use your powers for good, too."

"Wherever there's a need, that's where you'll find me," Khai intoned, standing with his legs akimbo, miming a perfect superhero.

"Oh yeah," Hollis muttered. "He's a regular boy scout.

Apparently someone was still miffed about being tased. I snickered, and Hollis glared at me.

"Sparky!" Jules exclaimed. "You've got your trail name, Khai."

"I guess I do," he mused.

"Just make sure you continue putting it to good use," I scolded him with mock seriousness. "You know, with great power-"

"Comes great idiocy," Hollis taunted.

"Oh yeah? You wanna go?" Khai laughed. "I promise I'll go easy on you this time."

Hollis jumped up, looking happy at the prospect of more exercise.

"Seriously?" Jules said. "Aren't you guys the least bit tired from today?"

"Nope," they both answered, grinning at each other as they settled into sparring stances.

I rolled my eyes. "No powers, you two," I reminded them.

"Yes, Mom," they said, and then they were off. Jules put the pot of food in the fire to simmer, and leaned back, clearly enjoying the show.

Me?

I'd seen it all before. I shook my head, smiling, and walked away to change out of my bathing suit and into some better clothes for the evening. The sun was starting to set and temperatures were dropping.

Our first day on the trail was coming to an end. There were things I wanted to write down in our trail journal, and a peaceful tiredness was beginning to steal over my body, relaxed from the walking and my time in the water.

It had been a perfect day, and I was looking forward to the next one.

Chapter 14

We broke camp early the next morning and made our way back to the trail. The hiking was pleasant, and we spent most of the time in our own thoughts, walking quietly through the woods. Every so often, we'd pass other hikers, some laden down with packs like us, others clearly just out for the day. Jules, the most extroverted of our group, liked to talk, so she spent her time engaging each of us in conversation in turn.

Walking with me, our exchange had taken a more serious turn. It had started out pleasantly enough, easy banter about what we would do when we got to Montreal, how other kids in our class were spending their summer, that sort of thing. But I'd seen her staring at Hollis ten yards ahead, and I couldn't help thinking of what Khai had said, how her infatuation would end with tears. More concerned about my friend than any bet I had made, I couldn't help saying something.

"Are you sure you want Hollis to notice you, anyways? I mean, you've seen the way he treats other girls."

Jules looked at me, offended. "He doesn't treat anyone badly. He just hasn't been ready to settle down."

"Right," I said slowly. "So what if he finally notices you, that way, and still doesn't want to settle down?"

"I-" She paused, shook her head. "He wouldn't treat me like that. It's different with us. I get him. He gets me. We're perfect for each other."

And there it was. The center of the delusion around which Jules had built her infatuation. I couldn't see any good way to correct it. And who was to say I should? At least I'd tried to warn her.

"Okay. I just don't want to see you get hurt, that's all."

"Don't worry about me. I can take care of myself," she said, squaring her shoulders.

"I know." And I did. The whole time we'd been planning this trip, I'd known what she was planning, too. The slow, grand seduction of Hollis Ward. Gods help us all.

"Hmph," she snorted. "You better. Whatever, I'm gonna go check on Khai, he's lagging pretty far behind."

I turned, and she was right. Khai was nowhere in sight.

"Want me to go with you?" I asked.

"Nah. I'm good." She jogged back down the hill we'd been climbing without another word. If she were anyone else I'd be worried I'd offended her, but Jules was tough, and she didn't hold grudges. If she was mad at me, it'd blow over by the time we made camp.

At least, that's what I'd thought.

She'd pretty much ignored me the rest of the day, and set up her hammock on the other side of the shelter, well away from me. Now, as twilight was sinking into the forest air, she volunteered to walk with Hollis to forage for white pine to make some vitamin C-rich tea.

I sat with Khai, stirring our night's dinner, some rehydrated vegetarian tikka masala. We'd decided to stay at the newly-rebuilt Melville Nauheim shelter, settling in quickly. A group of guys in their late twenties had already claimed the small 3-sided construction as their home for the evening, but we'd decided it would be nice to meet more people, and set up camp nearby. Plus, the shelter boasted a fresh water source and outhouse, welcome amenities at the end of the day.

Khai took over stirring, while I unpacked my journal and recorded the events of the day – minus my tiff with Jules.

I was just finishing when one of the men came over.

"Smells good, whatcha cooking?" he asked, sniffing the air.

"Tikka Masala." Khai looked up with an open smile, affable as always. "I'm Sparky, this is Ana. You hiking the AT?"

The man shook his head, pushing a strand of blonde hair out of his face. "Nah, we're heading north on the Long Trail. Name's David. What about you?"

"Same, heading north. Planning to finish in Montreal."

"That's cool." David nodded. "We're actually looking for some friends of ours, headed out over a month ago, no one's heard from them since."

"Wow, really?" I asked. "Are you talking about that couple that went missing in May?"

"Yeah." He squatted down next to me and poked at the ground with a stick. "The girl is Clarise, a cousin of mine. She was out on the trail with her boyfriend – those guys are some of his friends. When they called off the official search, we decided to do some investigating of our own. You haven't seen anyone like them, have you? Clarise and Tom? Tall, blonde girl and skinny Asian dude?"

"No," Khai and I answered at the same time. A wave of sadness washed over me. I felt so bad for this guy.

"Yeah. I figured. Still, gotta ask everyone." He shrugged, tried to put on a bright face.

"Didn't they go missing further north?" Khai asked.

"Yeah. We're following their route. Staying where they stayed, stopping where they stopped, right up until they stopped checking in that last day. Hoping for some kind of lead, you know?"

I nodded, not sure what to say.

"Sounds like a good plan," Khai said. "I hope you find them."

"I'm not sure I want to, you know," David said in a quiet voice. "I mean, at this point... I'd rather imagine them living their life out in secret somewhere, exploring the world off-grid on some hippie commune or something. Even a cult. Anything so long as they're still alive. My Aunt Suzie's already assumed the worst. Clarise's mom – she thinks they're dead."

"Wow, that's really rough," I said, placing my hand on his arm for support.

"Tell me about it," he agreed. "But enough about me. What about you all? Where you guys from?"

"Not too far from here, actually," I said, ignoring a warning look from Khai. "We live in Falls Depot."

I knew you weren't supposed to give out too much personal information to random strangers on the trail, but come on. This guy was pretty unlikely to be anyone dangerous.

"Oh, that's cool. So you've hiked the trail before?"

"Just short trips. Never the whole LT."

"Right on. Well, I'm from Philadelphia, more of city guy, myself. The guys I'm with are all more experienced hikers,

I'm hoping they'll keep me out of trouble," he said, making a face.

I laughed. "How's it going so far?"

"Not bad. No blisters, at least. I've been wearing these boots for two weeks around the city trying to break them in. Drove my boss at work crazy."

"Oh yeah? What do you do?"

"I'm a staffer at the Mayor's office, nothing glamourous. But they do expect me to wear a suit."

"I bet they loved the boots."

"The mayor said if I'm still wearing them when I get back from the trip, she'll burn them herself. She's kind of a fashionista."

Khai laughed. "I've seen her on TV, I think. She does like to dress up. She's really into the new science initiative the Senate has been pushing, right?"

"Yep. Philly's going to be one of the pilot cities for the new program."

"What's the program?" I asked, having no clue.

"They want to bring more fae science into schools, see what new things young minds can cook up," Khai explained.

"Oh, that sounds cool, I guess."

"Don't mind her," Khai said to David. "Ana's really not into science."

"No?" David asked. I shook my head, confirming Khai's statement.

"Me neither," David smiled at me. "I'm more of a history buff. Everything the fae have brought to this world in the last few decades – the advances we've made are amazing.

And the change of humanity since The Flare, well, you know how it is."

"Yeah, it's pretty amazing," I grinned. My fae heritage wasn't something I usually broadcasted, not because people judged you – that didn't happen much these days – but because I didn't really feel all that un-human. Plus, once people found out who my mother was, the attention could get a little overwhelming. Celebrity parents, and all that.

Hollis and Jules came back into camp laughing and smiling, Jules brandishing several small white pine branches, Hollis cradling something in his shirt.

"Hey Legs, Holl. About time!" Khai called, waving them over. "Guys, this is David." He moved the tikka masala to the side to sit and continue rehydrating now that it had been heated, and filled another pot with water for the tea.

"Sparky and Legs, huh? You guys got trail names already?" David asked quietly, with a bit of envy in his voice.

"Not all of us. You can probably guess which one is Legs," I laughed.

"Right," he nodded, "not much mystery there. And Sparky? How'd that name come about?"

I opened my mouth to explain but Khai put a hand on my arm.

"Let me," he grinned, a flash of light sparking in his eye.

He held out his hand, palm up. The air shimmered for a moment above it, and then a ball of fire formed, hovering harmlessly inches above his dark skin. Then it constricted, consolidating into a tiny ball of blue that shimmered and burst out into the evening air in all directions, like it was seeking a target. Seeking ground.

"Whoa, cool!" David whistled. "Nice party trick! So, you're fae?"

"Yeah," Khai nodded. He closed his hand with a flourish, and the ball of lightning disappeared.

"That's pretty awesome." David turned to me. "What about you? Are you fae, too?"

I nodded, tucking my hair behind one ear to show off the slight point at its tip. "But I can't do anything like that. I don't really have any active powers."

"Oh, that's too bad. But I hear fae abilities can take a while to develop sometimes, right? I know people like that."

"So they say," I sighed.

"And you guys?"

"Hollis, my brother, he's got a whole bunch of earth abilities. And Jules is human. Though she's kind of super-human when it comes to running sports...So, you know other fae?"

"A few, yeah. Not well. I've got such a big family, there's never been much need to look for other friends, especially once I left school. But I'm really glad to have met you guys." He lowered his voice conspiratorially, leaning in towards me. "Tom's buddies are all a bit more serious than I'm used to."

"Oh, they should meet Hollis, then, they'll get along fine," I smirked.

"Hey," Hollis protested beside me. "I object!"

"See what I mean?" I said, rolling my eyes. "Even around the campfire you manage to sound like a teacher, Holl."

"I know how to have a good time," he grumbled.

"I know you do, bro. I'm just kidding." I sighed.

"Don't feel bad, Hollis," Jules murmured playfully, rubbing his arm. "I always have fun when you're around."

"Thanks, Jules," Hollis said warmly. "Me, too."

Khai snorted and I smothered a laugh. Jules was laying it on a bit thick. I decided to distract myself from the flirtation playing out by serving up dinner.

"David, would you like some?" I offered him a plate.

"No, thanks, I already ate. You guys go ahead."

"Suit yourself," I said with a shrug, and handed the food to Khai, who passed it around the circle. We did this two more times, and then I was serving myself. The fare was good – spicy and wholesome. Simple, but on the trail, everything tasted like a three-star meal. Something about eating outside had always pleased me. Everything had more flavor after a day spent in the fresh air. It was like each cell in my body was fulfilled, not just my stomach.

I watched the others eat, and felt my contentment overflow onto the rest of them. Everyone was giving themselves entirely to their food, and silence descended upon the group.

I looked at David, and caught him watching me with a grin.

"What?"

"You're humming. You sing to yourself while you eat."

"I do not."

"Actually, you do," Khai laughed though a mouth full of food. "When you really like it."

"What?" I looked around the circle for confirmation, and watched Jules and Hollis both nod their heads in agreement.

"Oh yeah." "Totally."

Huh. Well. That was embarrassing. "Why hasn't anyone ever said anything?" I asked. I mean jeez, it's not like I was a toddler.

"It's cute." Khai shrugged.

"I figured you knew," Jules said, trying to smother a smile.

I looked at Hollis. "Don't look at me. You and Mom both do it. You can't tell me you've never noticed."

I thought back, chagrined. I really hadn't.

Hollis laughed. "Wow, you haven't, huh? Well, at least you don't rock back and forth like she does when she has chocolate cake."

I glared at him. "You are a terrible brother."

He cracked up, and I couldn't help it. So did I. Then, realizing this might quickly degenerate into an unwanted trail name, I changed the topic, steering conversation towards the next few day's plans. We'd hiked this area enough times on day trips to have no interest in any nearby side trails. The view from the fire tower on the top of Glastenbury Mountain? Seen it. The quaint little beaver pond nearby? I had photos galore of the large, toothy mammals. We'd be hiking through, aiming for areas with a bit more to offer our jaded eyes.

David sat quietly, smiling at our group's easy banter, until his crowd called him back for their own planning session. I imagined theirs would be a grimmer affair. How could it not be, when what you sought was most likely dead, already lost. The thought made me sad, and as if in answer, I heard a rumble of thunder in the distance.

Quickly, I checked my watch, which came equipped with basic weather warnings. No rain, no storms in the area. The thunder was an anomaly, nothing to worry about. Which I was glad for, because I wasn't in the mood to put up my tent, not now that I was full, and content. Determined to enjoy the rest of the night, I smiled at my friends and relaxed.

Everything was perfect.

Chapter 15

Everything sucked. The rain sucked. The mud sucked. The trail sucked.

After four days of gorgeous hiking weather, we'd been subjected to three miserable days of relentless rain. The first day, it hadn't really bothered me. I mean, every day couldn't be perfect. But after rolling down a hill in a stream of mud, I'd given in. At this point, I felt like I had become one with the rain, like the sky was crying my own tears, just for me. I know, I know, I was seriously wallowing in a fountain of self-pity. I tried to resist, but I couldn't help it. The more the rain fell, the more dejected I became. This morning, when I'd awoken to another forecast for "summer showers" I'd started crying. Seriously. Real tears and everything.

Hollis had teased me, saying I was going to make it rain even more if I didn't stop, which of course just made me cry harder. In the end, he'd thrown an arm around me, soothing me. "Don't worry, Rain, everything's going to be okay, you'll see. How about we hike out of here this afternoon and stay at the new hotel at Stratton Mountain? Tamarack Lodge?"

I'd nodded, wiping my eyes. "I'd like that."

And that was it.

That is how it happened.

Khai overheard our exchange and I had my trail name. Rain. The very thing I hated most about the trail, and it was my gods-be-damned name. Have I mentioned how much I hate my brother sometimes?

At that moment, though, I was loving him, because he had given me something to look forward to. Something dry. Something warm. I picked up my feet and marched on with renewed vigor, overtaking Jules and leading the way down the trail.

After all, there was no time to waste. A shower was calling my name. Oh, and a wash of clothes. Honest to goodness dry air without water in it.

Oh gods. I couldn't wait.

Soon, I had outpaced the group by over a quarter mile. I wouldn't say I was happy exactly. I wasn't singing in the rain or anything like that. But I had purpose now. Motivation. A goal.

I hiked the rest of the way alone. I assume everyone else stopped for lunch. Not me. I walked straight through, never breaking stride, my pace as relentless as the rain no matter how lightly it was falling now.

At the top of Stratton Mountain, I breathed a sigh of relief. In the distance, I could see a break in the clouds, a small slit of sunshine cutting through. But that's not what made me smile.

The gondolas were running. The big, huge, totally enclosed, *dry* gondolas. Thank goodness for mountain bikers, the bread and butter of ski mountains in the summer months. I let out a whoop and straightened my pack, jogging awkwardly towards the lift. In two minutes, I was riding the gondola down the mountain, a stupid grin on my face, a family of tourists snapping pictures of a faint rainbow in the distance as we descended.

By the time we got to the bottom, the rains had stopped and I emerged into the clear, humid air of summer. I walked over to the lodge, arranged two rooms with double beds for our little group, took one of the room keys and made for the shower like a bear after honey. I was determined to focus all my efforts on running through the shower's hot water supply before switching to the more conventional sonic wave mode, and the front desk had promised they would hold the keys for when the others got there, whenever that would be.

By the time I came out, the bathroom was filled with an impenetrable fog scented with roses and lemons. It was pure, unadulterated bliss. I reveled in the soft fullness of the hotel robe, my first real luxury in a week, and sighed.

I loved the hiking, really, I did. Mostly. But this? It was perfection. I opened the door to the room and found Jules sitting on the floor, emptying her pack.

"About time. I was beginning to think you'd melted in there."

"If I could melt, I would have done that days ago." I laughed, toweling off my hair. It was amazing how something like a little hot water could completely change one's perspective.

"Oh my god, it laughs!" Jules crowed happily. "Glad to see you're still in there. You were starting to worry me, honestly. I don't think I've ever seen you so miserable."

"I know, right? I guess I'm not quite as tough as I'd like to be." I shrugged, not really caring. At this point, I wasn't sure anything could bother me. Maybe part of me had melted in that shower, because I felt more at peace than I had in... Well, maybe ever.

"Hmm." Jules looked me over, as if examining me for cracks. "Okay. Well, I am glad you are getting back to your usual self. I was just sorting out the things I'd take to launder. Which seems to be almost everything, unfortunately. How about you?"

I rummaged through my pack. "I think I have one serviceable pair of shorts and a tank top left, that's about it." I pulled on the dry clothes and added the rest to Jules pile. "Why don't you go get cleaned up, and I'll take these down to the machines?"

"That'd be awesome, thanks. Do you think you left me any hot water?"

"Oh, there may be a couple of minutes worth left." I winked at her and gathered the clothes up into my arms, dumping them into the laundry basket the Lodge had thoughtfully provided. The woman at the desk had told me there was a laundry room on the first floor, by the locker rooms for the pool and spa. I slid my feet into the one-size-fits-all hotel slippers, too large for my feet, and walked into the hall.

It felt so strange to be treading on thick carpet, under a ceiling. No birds. No rain. No sky. No dirt. It was kind of miraculous, yet foreign. It's strange, how quickly the modern mind adapts to life on the outside, the wild life, as if it is all one has ever known. A symptom of our natural origins, perhaps, a device of our innate functioning systems, that we are, at heart, wild, too.

I found the laundry machines, set the clothes to heavy washing and drying, and sat down to wait. A hotel phone sat on the small table nearby, so I picked it up, deciding to give my parents a ring.

"Hello?"

"Hey, Dad. It's me, Ana."

"Ana! I saw you guys hit the hotel a while ago. Everything okay? Nobody's hurt, are they?"

"No, no, we're all fine. The rain was getting to be a bit much for all of us, so we decided to take a break. Dry off, wash our clothes, you know."

No need to admit that I was the one who had inspired our little vacation from the trail.

"Ah, yes, it has been pretty steady the last few days, hasn't it? Even the fleet are staying inside."

"Yeah, well, smart unicorns."

"Well, earlier this morning they were forecasting another couple days of rain, but now they are saying that the rain should break by this evening, and there are no big storm systems coming in that I can see. So you're in luck. How about everything else? You having a good time? You guys have enough food? Money? Your gear holding up okay?"

"Yeah, Dad, we're fine. Everything's great. These new pack meals weigh so little, I think we have enough food between us to last the whole summer without leaving the trail."

My dad laughed, a nervous kind of a bark. "Right. Well, don't go doing anything like that."

"What, afraid we'll never come back?" I teased.

"Always," my dad answered seriously.

"Dad," I said, rolling my eyes.

"I know, I know. Over protective. Alright. So what else? Any good stories?"

"Well, we got our trail names. Khai is Sparky, Jules is Legs, I'm Rain, and Hollis is Mr. Perfect."

"Rain, huh? How'd you get that one?"

"Hollis. Just because I was tired of all the rain," I grumbled, trailing off. "And Khai, well, you can guess what he was doing."

"I can imagine. You tell Khai to be careful, we don't want any forest fires starting on his account."

"I'll be sure to remind him," I said, grinning.

"Good. Well, I don't want to keep you. I'm sure you want to enjoy your time off the trail. Too bad your mom's out, I know she'd love to hear your voice."

"How about you guys? You having a good trip?"

"Oh yeah, it's gorgeous here. We've got a great hotel, and your mom has found a dessert vendor at the market that she might actually leave me for. That's where she is right now, getting more treats for breakfast. Tell Hollis to give us a call later, okay?"

"Okay, Dad. Love you."

"I love you, too, baby."

I hung up the phone, and watched the laundry spinning in the machine, flashes of light marking the sanitization phase. Another couple minutes, and they'd be dry, ready to wear.

I zoned out on the machine, the ever changing colors luring me into a meditative state. When the timer buzzed, I jumped a little, surprised. Embarrassed, I looked around, but no one was nearby to see. I'd always been like that, easily surprised. Hollis had always been the opposite – unshakeable. He didn't just have earth powers, he was a rock. Sometimes I wondered if that was why my own powers refused to manifest – was I just not grounded enough? Not earthy enough to deserve them?

I shook my head. Foolish thoughts. Powers came when they were ready. Mine would, too, soon enough. In the meantime, being a healer was pretty cool. And studying techniques with Airmed was sure to be a blast. Maybe she would even be able to help me unlock my other abilities, assuming I even had them.

I emptied the contents of the machine back into my basket and headed back upstairs, already planning how to enjoy the rest of our day in paradise.

Chapter 16

You would think that after days of rain, the last thing I would want to do would be to get wet.

And you'd be right. But you'd also be wrong.

Getting wet and muddy in a cold summer rain? No, thank you.

Immersing myself in a soothing hot tub, followed by some laps in a heated pool? Yes, please.

After watching an old teen movie on TV, Jules and I had headed down to the pool to relax. The hot tub was exactly what I'd needed. It was like every last grain of dirt that had even ever thought about attaching itself to me had finally been cleansed. I felt pure and radiant. It was bliss. Eventually, Jules dragged me out, saying that I was turning pink like a lobster, citing some silly 30-minute rule that was posted on the wall. I tried to argue, but I was too limp to resist as she and Khai hauled me out and dumped me unceremoniously into the pool.

I came up spluttering.

"What!? You guys are cruel!"

"Sorry, sis, you can blame me," Hollis laughed, shaking back his own wet hair. "I put them up to it."

"Of course, Mr. Perfect strikes again." Too relaxed to care, I fell back into the water, floating with a dopey grin on my face. Life was good. Better than good. It was perfect.

Jules swam over and looked down at me. "Wanna swim some laps?"

"Sure, why not?" It actually felt weird to be so inactive, after walking so much every day.

"Sweet! First one to do twenty laps cooks dinner tomorrow!" Jules taunted as she took off.

"You're on!" I dove after her, knowing I'd never catch her. Longer legs, longer arms. Jules had more body, more athlete bits, working in her favor. But it didn't mean I couldn't try.

I eased into a steady crawl, setting a good pace. Fast, but not so fast that I couldn't maintain it. For now, Jules was only ten feet ahead. If I could at least maintain my distance, I wouldn't feel too bad at the end.

With that goal in mind, I erased all thoughts from my mind, just allowing myself to enjoy the feel of the water as I sluiced through it, waves sheeting off my skin as I lifted my arm out of the water. The softness of the surface of the pool as I lowered it back in. Kicking right, kicking left. The pattern of my body's movements joining with the gentle motion of the water. Laps went by, one after the other, a simple repetition of motion and time. All the same.

The hot tub really had done me a world of good, because as I swam I didn't feel tired at all. I felt energized. Fresh, and free. Swimming was easier than ever, almost as if the liquid was making me lighter. I hit the wall, the end of the last lap, and stopped. I felt great.

I looked around, expecting to see Jules grinning at me, but she wasn't there. The sound of skin on water had me turning, and I saw her, a good twenty feet behind me. Yet to finish.

A few moments, and her hand was slapping the wall next to mine.

"Wow. Good time, Ana!" she said, surprised. "All that hiking's really paid off, I guess."

"I know, right? Or you're more tired than you thought."

She shrugged. "I feel good. I think you must've developed some extra upper body strength, that's all. Good for you!"

This was why I loved Jules, why she'd always been my best friend. She was so positive, so easy. She was the perfect match to my more careful ways.

"I love you," I laughed, hugging her.

"Whoa girl, I love you, too. You feeling okay?"

"Yeah, I just, I don't know. I'm just really glad you're my friend, you know? I'm sorry about those things I said before, you know, about you and Hollis."

"I know. I'm sorry, too. I shouldn't have gotten so mad."

"No, you were right. I was being a jerk."

"How about this, we're both jerks, okay?"

"Okay," I agreed, giving her another hug.

"You girls need some privacy?" Hollis drawled from above.

"Nope, we're good!" Jules squeaked and widened her eyes at me before diving back under the water. I watched her swim away, and bit back a smile.

"How much of that did you hear?" I asked, looking up at my brother while he wrapped a towel around his hips.

"How much of what? All I know is you two were having some sort of emo-fest over here, and Khai and I are hungry. You ready to get out, get dinner?"

I sighed with relief. "Of course, sounds great. I'm starved, actually. Meet you at the pub in half an hour?"

Hollis didn't bother answering, just nodded and walked off, meeting Khai at the door to the lobby.

I rounded up Jules and told her of the plan. A short shower later and some dry clothes, and we were sitting in the Irish-themed pub, ordering drinks and looking over menus.

Ah, menus. Glorious appetizers. Bar burgers. Chocolatey fudge drenched desserts. I felt like I was at a fancy restaurant, everything seemed like such a treat. I couldn't wait for dessert.

I wasn't the only one, either. My good mood was contagious, or maybe it was just that everybody else had been yearning for some respite from the rain as much as I had. Either way, as I looked around the table, I noticed that we were all grinning like fools.

At least we weren't drooling, I thought.

Khai's eyes met mine above his menu. "What's so funny?"

"Nothing," I answered honestly. "I'm just so happy to be here."

"Me, too," he said, smiling. He closed his menu and leaned back in his chair. "The trail's been great, but this is like paradise."

"Right? That's exactly what I've been thinking."

"I know, me, too," Jules agreed.

Hollis put his menu to the side and grinned at us. "Wow, aren't you guys a bunch of easy dates? Good to know this is all it takes to make you girls happy."

"Hey," Khai said, swatting Hollis. "I object to your use of pronouns."

"Hey man, I don't judge. Your gender is totally cool with me, no matter what you decide in the end."

"I bet. It's okay Hollis, don't worry. We all know you've been holding out for Khai all these years."

"I don't- What-" Hollis sputtered, and the rest of us laughed.

"Though frankly, I'm not sure you deserve him," I finished, putting my hand over Khai's. "Even if he does light your fire.

Jules snorted. "Nice one."

I winked at her, and was saved from thinking up something else clever to say by the waitress delivering our drinks. Which was good, because I was pretty sure I'd run dry on both counts. Khai turned his hand over in mine, giving it a warm squeeze, before letting go and picking up his beer.

We'd always played it this way. Hollis and Khai were bros, but Khai and I also presented a united front against Hollis' shatter-proof ego and superior ways. I mean, you couldn't let that sort of thing go unchecked. Too much perfection just wasn't healthy, in my opinion.

We placed our orders, Hollis bantering with the waitress in his typical easy way. If she was like most girls, he'd have a date set up by the end of the meal. I watched Jules, hoping she wasn't bothered, but she didn't even seem to be paying attention to the flirting that was going on. Catching my glance, she leaned forward.

"So, how psyched are you to get to Montreal, huh? I mean, the trail is cool and all, but tonight I'm remembering just how much I like civilization."

"I know, right? It'll be nice to get to the city. I love it there in the summer, it's so happy. But I think I'm even more excited to go study with Airmed after."

"You're studying with Airmed?" Khai asked, surprised. "When did that happen?"

"Oh, at graduation!" I exclaimed. "Mialloch Airron gave me an official invitation from her himself. Mom's totally jealous. I'm supposed to go straight to Aeden after we get to Montreal."

Khai's left eyebrow had lowered, the way it usually did when he didn't like what he was hearing. "Right away?"

"No, not right away," I said, shrugging. "Whenever I'm ready, really. But I don't want to wait too long, there's only so much time before school starts up."

"So, this Airmed, she does what, exactly? I mean, your mom is an amazing healer. What can Airmed teach you?" Jules said, popping a piece of cornbread in her mouth.

"Are you serious?" Hollis scoffed. "Airmed's an Ancient. She knows everything there is to know about healing. She's regrown limbs, for gods' sakes."

"Really? Well, I never heard of her." Jules lifted one shoulder and turned to me, barely paying attention to Hollis.

"She's kind of antisocial. Which is why it's such a big deal that she wants to teach me. Though I guess I shouldn't be surprised, she is good friends with Jade, and Mialloch is one of my dad's best friends from when they were kids. Still. I'm definitely lucky she wants to spend time with me at all."

"So, you'll be learning how to grow fingers and stuff? I guess that could come in handy." She wiggled her eyebrows and we all groaned at the bad pun.

"Maybe... I know she works a lot with flower essences, herbs and stuff like that. She taught my mom some stuff about working with honey. So we might just study that kind of stuff. I don't know, really."

"Well, that's cool. Maybe you can make me something for sore muscles when I'm training."

"Something like that would come in handy now, actually," Khai mused, rubbing his neck. "Carrying that pack is making me work on muscles I didn't know I had."

Jules laughed. "Truer words were never spoken."

Hollis stretched. "Yeah, my shoulders have been killing me."

"Seriously? Mr. Perfect feels pain?" I teased. "I didn't know it was possible."

"Shut it, you," he said good-naturedly. "I never said I was perfect."

"Oh no, not you. Just that group of girls from Holyoke, and the Girl Scout troop, and that doctor's wife, and-"

Hollis blushed, a rare occurrence. Jules folded her hands under her chin and fluttered her eyelashes, crooning.

"Oh, so you must be the Mr. Perfect we've been hearing so much about on the trail," she said in a heavily accented Dutch falsetto, mimicking the doctor's wife we'd met two nights ago, Mrs. Harding. "I thought everyone must be exaggerating, but no, you are perfect, are you not, Mr. Perfect?"

Jules blinked up at him, doe-like, reenacting the first time we had heard Hollis' trail name, a dubbing he had received in absentia, as girls left in his wake gossiped amongst themselves, apparently.

"She did not do that," Hollis gritted out, annoyed.

"Did not do what?" Jules asked, staying in character as she ran a hand along the muscles on his arm. "Did not rub your arm, like this? Did not ask you if there was anything you weren't," she paused, licking her lips, "skilled at?"

"Jules," Hollis warned.

"Did she not?" Jules blinked, and phased out of character, suddenly becoming Jules again in demeanor and voice. "Get over yourself, Hollis. It's just a trail name."

"An embarrassing one," he grumbled.

"What's that, sweetie?" The sugary voice of our server intruded as she placed a massive bleu cheese burger in front of Hollis.

"Nothing, thanks."

"Okay," she said, looking a bit put out before she pasted on a polite smile. "Another round of drinks?"

"Yes, please, that would be great," Jules answered, smiling up at her. "That will be just, perfect."

Chapter 17

"So," I whispered to Jules, looking around to make sure that the boys were out of earshot. "What happened last night? Hollis can barely look at you."

"I know. Isn't it great?" Jules sighed, a huge smile lighting up her face.

"Um... I don't know. Is it?"

We were back on the trail, freshly showered and laundered, well rested and filled to the brim with fresh tea and an amazing assortment of baked goodies from the morning's breakfast buffet. In short? I was a very happy hiker. But I'd turned in early, as had Khai, leaving Jules and Hollis playing billiards in the lounge. Something had changed between them, and I wanted to know what.

"Well, you know, we played pool for a while, and that was fun. Then Hollis was complaining about his shoulder again, blaming his poor shots on that, so I offered to give him a back rub."

I raised my eyebrows at her. "A back rub?"

"Yeah, that's it, I swear." She laughed. "I mean, I may have leaned in a little while I did it, breathed in his ear a bit, you know. But I swear, nothing happened."

"Well, something happened."

"I know, right? I think he's really finally starting to see me as a real girl, not just some annoying little sister type. No offense."

"Trust me, none taken. I am eternally thankful that Hollis sees me only as a sister." I shuddered, gagging to think of the alternative. "Blech."

"Right, well." She laughed, shaking her head at me. "Like I said, I think I'm making real progress. Did you see his face at dinner last night every time I pretended to be that Dutch woman? Well, I did it some more while we were playing pool, I think that's actually what messed up some of his shots."

"Hollis never misses a shot," I mused in disbelief.

"He does now," she snorted. "I actually won the last game, can you believe it?"

I looked at my friend with the respect she deserved. "You know, I can. I take everything I ever said about your crush on my brother back. I think you're going to be really good for him, however it turns out. Who knows, maybe someday we'll even be sisters, for real."

"That would be so cool. Your parents are way more chill than mine. And we could finally take that trip to Aeden we're always talking about."

"Why wait? You should come with me when I go to see Airmed."

"Aw, wish I could. But my parents already sprung for that 6-week soccer camp that the university wanted all the new recruits to attend. It's supposed to really up my game, or build team spirit, or something like that."

"As if you need any help in either department. I can't believe you're going to be doing track and soccer all year. Who's going to veg out with me every afternoon?"

"Yeah, right. You're going to be so busy reading every book in that damn library, I bet it'll be me having to drag you out, and not the other way around."

I laughed. "You're probably right."

"Jules seems to be right a lot of the time, lately."

Hollis' voice took us both by surprise. He and Khai had managed to catch up with us without either of us noticing. Hopefully, they hadn't heard any of our earlier conversation.

Jules recovered quickly, retorting, "I'm always right."

"Ha!" Khai laughed. "Like that time when you bet us that if you ate a tiny leaf of poison ivy, you'd be immune to the mature leaves for the rest of the season?"

"Hey, that's what they said on the internet. Apparently, everybody does it down south. Maybe our ivy is different up here, more potent."

"Or what about that time she told Ana that you could use club soda instead of baking soda to make a volcano for science class?" Hollis laughed, elbowing Khai in the ribs.

"Hey, I was what, eight? I thought they were the same thing. I wasn't that far off."

"Not far off?" I hooted. "Girl, the whole volcano dissolved all over the floor before I could even put the vinegar in."

"Well, no one ever said it was a good idea to build the mountain out of flour." She crossed her arms, biting her cheek as she hid a smile.

"It was Papier Mache." I laughed, protesting.

"Whatever."

And that's how it was. The rest of the day, and the ones that followed. By the end of our second week we'd passed the AT/Long Trail split, explored several amazing side trails, found some stellar waterfalls and only had one more day of rain. Our group was as close as ever, everyone getting along great. Jules and Hollis spent a lot of time together on the trail, often forging ahead like the natural leaders they both were. Were they flirting? Not enough that I was sure I'd win my bet, but that was okay. Something better was happening – they were becoming real friends. The bond that Hollis, Khai and I all shared had grown to encompass Jules in a way it never had before, and I was happy for my friend. Happy that the guys weren't just treating her like my annoying little friend anymore, but an equal.

I couldn't help it. It gave me the warm and fuzzies. Knowing we'd all be at school together the next year made it that much better, too. Nothing made me happier than when everyone was getting along. The best part of my week? I hadn't cried once.

Maybe it was the healer in me. I don't know. All I knew was the more fun they had, the better I felt.

Two weeks in, and we were about halfway through the Long Trail. Since we'd split off from the AT, we'd been seeing fewer hikers. Sure, there were the occasional day-trippers and some thru-hikers, but as we headed further north into rougher, less-populated country, the social hubbub of the AT seemed very far away. Things were quiet, and we'd taken to heading off trail more and more, exploring the wilds.

Which is why, when presented with a particularly nice afternoon, we decided to hike a side trail towards a secret spot we'd heard about from a friend of my dad's. There was an old barn foundation cut into the ground, which made for a nice, clear shelter in the woods. Nearby, there was even supposed to be a mill site, part of the ancient farm, where you could bathe in the runoff under a small waterfall.

We made camp, finding the ruins of the barn as cozy as Jonas had said it would be, and everyone settled in to read or nap. Me? I wasn't in the mood for resting. I was aching for that bath. I checked the coordinates for the old mill and entered it into my GPS watch, smiling as a small arrow appeared in the upper corner of the screen to guide my way.

I stood up and announced my destination, promising I'd be back in an hour or two. Hollis muttered something about wearing my watch, and I held up my wrist for him to see as I left. Of course I had it – how else would I navigate to the falls? I shook my head, muttering as I stalked off. Did he really think I was that much of an idiot?

The woods were in full growth, the rains of early summer having given rise to a riot of green. Lush moss grew along rocks and trees, and the air was warm and thick with humidity. I walked uphill for several minutes, clambering over boulders and ducking under a fallen tree resting precariously against a large oak, until a charmed scene unfolded before me.

A large creek wound through the forest, flowing downhill past me. In its path, the unmistakable square box foundation of a mill still stood, complete with channels for the water to collect or flow, and a space where the wheel would have turned. Now, of course, it was long decayed, the wood fallen victim to both water and time. Above the mill house, a large pool collected the creek waters, creating the pressure that would have been needed to turn the wheel. Below, another deep pool glistened, clear and cool, disturbed only by the falling water from above.

The falls.

It was perfect, like something out of a storybook faerie garden.

I stripped out of my clothes slowly, reveling in the magic of the moment. The woods were so peaceful, so quiet. During all the time we'd been on the trail, it was rare that I would have time like this to myself. No matter what, someone was always nearby, or around the bend. But here? I was all alone. My friends were lazing about back at the camp, and there wasn't a trail within miles.

It was just me, the water, and the elementals. Surely, in a place like this, the spirits of the forest would be present in number. I said a quiet greeting, asking permission and giving thanks as I slipped into the water, the cool liquid shocking against my warm skin. Feeling welcomed at heart, I smiled and dove in, coming up across the pool, under the falling water.

It wasn't a large stream, just a foot or so across, flowing gently down over a lip of stones above, so that it came down in a sheet perfect for showering.

I don't know how long I stood there. The music of the water, the birdsong above, it lulled my thoughts into a place where time did not exist. It could have been half an hour, it may have been more. I should have been cold, probably, but I wasn't. The sun was warming the rocks around the pool, the stones in the mill, and radiating the heat onto my skin. My eyes were closed, but I could see it, sense it, the light coming through my lids like a kiss.

Through the warmth, a prickle of unease lit along my spine and opened my eyes. Something was making its way through the forest. Too loud for a bear, too quiet for a deer. I hoped it wasn't a wolf or a mountain lion, but trusted the water would keep me safe. I sank down into the water up to my chin, stepping behind the falls as I turned to see what had disturbed me.

Through the falling water, I saw the figure of a man passing between the trees. Something more dangerous than a lion, then. Even after The Flare, things happened sometimes. People's emotions got the better of them. Not like before, but despite its lack of wars and overall safety, the world was still a place to take care in. I sank lower into the pool.

"Ana! Where are you?"

I recognized the voice before I could see him clearly. Relief flooded me, and I swam out from behind my watery shield.

"Hey, Khai."

He stopped in his tracks a few feet away from the water's edge.

"What the hell, Ana? What are you doing out here all alone?"

"Well, you were sleeping, and everybody else wanted to read. So yeah, I came out by myself, so what?"

He looked down at the ground, noticing my clothes. "For gods' sake, are you naked?"

I giggled. "Yep."

"I could have been anyone. You can't just-"

"Oh, lighten up. I said where I was going, and I had my watch. It's not like I could get lost. And come on, you really think anyone is going to stumble across me here? In the middle of nowhere?"

"Jonas found it. I'm sure other people know where it is. The point it, you don't know. Soon, you're going to be at college, Ana, in a big city. You've got to learn to be more careful. It's just too dangerous for a girl like you to be-"

"A girl like me?"

What did he mean?

"You mean, a girl without powers? Or a girl that's small? Or maybe just a girl, period? Come on, Khai, tell me what you mean."

His lips clamped into a straight line and he crossed his arms over his chest, glaring at me. His gaze did not intimidate me.

I stared back, daring him to speak.

Instead, he sighed.

"No, that's not... Fine. Yes. All of that. Because you're you. Okay? You should always be prepared, for anything. But lately, you're just... I don't know, kissing random guys? Skinny dipping alone in the wilds of Vermont? How is any of that safe? What do you think your dad would do if he knew?"

"Oh, come on Khai. Seriously? He's my dad. Of course he'd flip. That doesn't mean I'm actually in any danger. I can't believe you think I'm that weak."

"It's not that, Ana. I just... You should have stayed at camp, okay, or at least brought Jules with you."

"Jules? Jules? You think Jules is stronger than me? Has she had years of training, like Hollis and me?"

He opened his mouth, and I kept talking. "You think she's better, just because she's bigger, or a little more coordinated? How dare you."

"No, I don't think that. But at least if you don't have powers, you can have safety in numbers."

There. He'd said it.

Like I was somehow *less than*, because I didn't have active powers. Like I needed to be protected, contained, saved.

Chapter 18

I felt like a tiger in a cage. Everyone wanted me to be the person they thought I was. Do this. Do that. Be helpless. Be safe.

But dammit, I was tired of being good. I was tired of being cautious.

"I don't need powers to keep me safe, Khai. I'm not helpless."

His eyes strayed from my face to the murky water just below my shoulders.

"I could have been anyone, Ana," he repeated. "You shouldn't be on your own like this."

"Like what? Oh, you mean naked?" I took a step forward, rising slightly out of the water as I did.

"Gods' blood, Ana," Khai swore, spinning in place to face away from me. "Stay in the water."

"But why? You said I shouldn't be swimming. So I'll get out." I laughed. "What's the matter, Khai? It's not like you haven't seen me naked before."

The last time had probably been in third grade.

"Are you afraid you'll like what you see?" I teased, my eyes unsmiling, despite the tilt of my lips. If I was a cat, my tail would have been flicking from side to side, a clear indication of my readiness to strike.

"No," Khai retorted. But he still didn't turn around. Totally annoyed, I brushed the water from my body and pulled on my clothes, the residual moisture making everything cling in a less than comfortable way. Yet another thing to be mad at Khai about, the jerk.

"Don't follow me. I don't want to see you or talk to you for at least an hour," I huffed, and brushed past him, jostling him out of my way with my shoulder.

"Ana," Khai said in a low, concerned voice.

The concern was the final straw.

"Make that two hours," I growled, and took off into the woods.

Even though I didn't quite have the rest of my family's trail running skills, it was still something I liked to do from time to time. Right now, though, it was more about pounding out my frustration with my feet, than anything else. I ran, and I ran hard.

After an hour, I looked down at my wrist, ready to program in the headings to get back to camp.

The wrist was bare. I'd taken off my watch when I'd gone swimming, and now...well, now I was somewhere in the woods, and I had no idea where. Crap. Hollis was going to kill me. Khai would probably gloat over how I'd proved him right. And me? Well, I needed to focus on getting back. I knew Hollis could probably use his earth powers to find me, but it would take time, and create more drama. If I could get back on my own, it would be better for everyone involved.

I turned around and started walking, hoping I could trace my route back.

After twenty minutes, I knew I was lost. Nothing looked familiar at all. My frustration turned to real anger, anger at myself, anger at Khai, anger at just about everything I could think of. I sat on a rock, fuming, going over everything in my mind that was so unfair, so upsetting.

Too small. No powers. Too nice. Too sheltered. Too clumsy. And now – lost.

Thunder rumbled nearby, and I looked up, surprised. The sunny skies of the afternoon had given way to an ominous dark green sky. I looked around, and winced. No good stones or caves for hiding in. No pack to squat on, either. So much for that tidbit of advice from Dad. Lightning flashed overhead and the rain broke, falling in huge drops all around me. I spooked, breaking into a run. If I was running, I'd be harder to hit, right?

I scanned the forest frantically for shelter, and almost missed the cliff that loomed ahead of me. Stopping at the last moment, hand propped against a tree on the edge, I panted for breath. Thirty feet below, in a small clearing there was some sort of encampment, complete with large canvas tents and several large wooden yurts.

Some people hurried from the tents towards the safety of the yurts, young men and women. They looked normal enough, clean cut and organized. They were probably part of some natural sciences research group.

Lightning and thunder cracked and boomed again, almost simultaneous, and sent me scurrying down the hill to the right of the stone ledge in a frenzy.

Whoever these people were, I hoped they had room for one more.

Chapter 19

I flung open the door to the closet yurt. I hadn't seen anyone heading in here, so I figured there must be more room.

Yeah, okay, not really. It was just the closest one, and the last bolt of lightning had struck close enough to smell the ozone.

I crashed through the door, eyes wide, water streaming down my face. Surely, I looked crazed. I plastered a smile on my face and looked around, ready to make friends.

And instead I found...

I didn't know what the hell I'd found. The walls of the circular structure were framed with cages. No, not cages. Jail cells. And they weren't empty.

"What the fu-"

"Ana?" The sound of my name, coming from one of the shadowed cells shocked me further.

I took a step forward, the building rumbling from yet another onslaught of thunder. At least it masked my own shaking.

"Who's there?"

Something rustled to my left, and a man limped forward, grasping the bars of his cage.

"It's me, David. Jesus, Ana, what are you doing here?"

"I. The storm. I-"

"Forget it kid, we don't have time for talking. Kid, see those keys, there on the wall?" A grizzled, grey-haired man asked me, pointing behind me. I turned to look, and nodded.

"Y-yeah?"

"These bastard warpers like to tease us by keeping them in plain sight. Now, how about you let us out."

"Right! Of course." I grabbed the keys, ran over to David's cell first. "David?" I asked quietly, working the key in the lock. "Are you okay? Is this okay?"

He seemed to understand my unspoken question. I mean, I knew David was a good guy, but these other people? I didn't want to let out some mass killers or illegal poachers or anything. "Yes, yes. Let everyone out. Please."

"Okay." I nodded, took a deep breath. "Okay."

And then I sprang into action, quickly opening each door. Eight cells, seven people.

"Quick, girl. Did anyone see you come in here?" The grey-haired man demanded.

"No. I don't think so. The storm outside... I think they're all in the other yurts."

"Good." Grey opened the door a crack and peered outside. "This storm is the perfect cover. They'll have a hard time tracking us in this. You, Ana, you have a camp nearby?"

"No. Maybe? I don't know. I got lost. I don't have my GPS."

"Figures," he grunted. "Alright, well, then, I say everybody split up into pairs, we fan out. They can't catch all of us."

The others nodded running off in separate directions. I turned towards the cliffs.

"This is the way I came. Can you run?" The thunder had stopped, and the rain seemed to be dying off.

"I'll do my best. My ankle, I think it's sprained."

"Crap. Okay, hold on." I walked him around the yurt, so the other buildings were hidden. At least if someone came outside, they wouldn't see us right away. I knelt down and put my hands around his ankle. There was definitely some heat and swelling there, but nothing I couldn't take care of. I reached out with my senses, feeling for the source energy of life flowing all around me, and pulled the energy through me, sending it out in pulses through my hands. In moments, the heat diminished. The swelling would take a few minutes to go down, but I could feel the cells doing their work, healing the body miraculously fast. Or, faetastically fast.

However you chose to look at it.

"Okay, you're good. Let's go." I stood up and grabbed his hand. David followed me, slack-jawed.

"I thought you said you don't have any active powers."

"I don't."

"Then what the heck was that?"

"I can heal things. Cells. You know."

"You're like a modern day Jesus, and you say it like it's no big deal."

I shrugged, climbing up the muddy hill as fast as I could. "It's not like that. I can't bring people back to the dead. No one can. I mean, don't me wrong, healing is cool, but it's not considered an active power. The few other healers I know have other abilities, too. Ones that go along with their element."

"Oh, right. Like earth, air, fire?"

"Exactly," I huffed, short of breath and still twenty feet from the top of the hill. I slipped, and David braced my leg, stopping my slide.

"Careful."

"I got it," I grumbled, pulling myself up the slippery slope by grasping hold of a young sapling.

For a while, we didn't talk. We got to the top of the hill and just ran. Moments later we heard shouts behind us, down below, which only made us run faster. If the people holding David had any outdoor skills at all, they would know we had come this way. Climbing and slipping up that hill of leaves and mud was sure to have left some conspicuous tracks, for anyone looking.

Fear pierced my heart, and I ran harder, and as I ran the rain fell harder, too. After twenty minutes, I had to stop, catch my breath. With any luck, our tracks had been blamed on the heavy rain, and no one was following us. Not that I was ready to give up yet.

"Let's walk for a minute, okay? Then we run again."

"Yeah, okay," David agreed, holding his side as we walked.

"So, you going to tell me what was going on back there? What happened to the guys you were hiking with? And who were all those people?"

"Warpers."

"What?"

"Warpers happened. Those people back there – that's what they call themselves."

"And the rest of you? Why were you in cages?"

"Warpers are... Crap. This is going to be hard to explain."

"Try me."

"Ok, well, you know how the fae are like humans, only...different?"

"Yeah?"

"Well, there are some other people who are different, too."

"The, what did you call them? Warpers?" I asked, anxiety rising in my chest. Were they like the Dark fae my parents had fought? Or some kind of new horrible mutation?

"Yes. Well, no. Some of the people are warpers, but not all of them. Not even most of them."

"David," I sighed, exasperated. "Get on with it. Break time is almost over."

"Right. Sorry. Okay. So some humans aren't entirely human."

"Are you talking about hybrids? With the fae?"

"Hybrids, yes. Fae, no. We're, um, well, we're part alien."

"I'm sorry, what?"

He laughed. "I know, it sounds crazy, right? But I've heard the fae histories of how your ancestors terraformed the earth, how you all believe you came from the stars, too, so hear me out, okay?"

"Okay..."

"So thousands of years ago, my ancestors came to this planet. The Nommo, or Star Walkers, visited earth, but only with their minds, not their bodies. They had greater abilities and intellects than our own. They traveled here as pure consciousness, taking over the minds of men, mutating their DNA to be more like their own and passing on special powers to humans while they used the human bodies. These enhanced humans had the powers of telekinesis, mind control through speech, and could create illusions or glamours that would fool the keenest eyes. Others gained the power of telepathy and astral travel like the Nommo themselves. You can find similar stories throughout the region of Middle East, in Sumeria, Turkey, Iraq. The Annunaki, the Nephilim."

"I've heard some of those stories," I said, thinking of my parents' work. "Go on."

"Well, those people whose bodies they used, they had children, and these kids grew up to have the powers of their fathers and mothers, too. As you can imagine, though, with all these powers, some people wanted more. More power. More control. Dominion over the regular humans who worshiped them as gods. You know. A great war broke out, and the Nommo left. Their Star Children were forced to hide their powers, control their greed, and slip under the radar of the rest of the world."

"So that's it? You're one of these star kids?"

"Yeah. Starseed, Star Child."

"And the warpers?"

"Starseeds who have fallen prey to their lust for power."

"Ah. But wait. How? I mean, the Dark fae all turned to the Light years ago. Humans stopped fighting their pointless wars. Why not you? I mean, not you, personally, but, the rest of you?"

"You mean The Flare? Your sun didn't affect us. Something in our DNA, we're not hardwired to respond the same way to the Light. Wherever the Nommo came from, whatever they are, they're different enough from the fae that your technology doesn't always work the same way on us."

"Whoa. That's crazy. I bet some scientists would love to figure out why."

"I bet you're right. Which, no offense, is another reason we usually keep our existence on the down low. Some people in government know about us, but as long as we keep the warpers under control, they leave us alone."

"And those guys back there?"

"Warpers, like I said. Some crazy fringe group that wants to recruit more of us to their side, and take over the country. I guess not everyone likes this world-topia you fae have created."

"Seriously? They *want* a war?"

"No. They want control, power. War is just a side effect of the process."

"But that's crazy."

"Um, hello, have you been listening to what I said? Since The Flare, people have been changing. Normal humans, getting powers. Some becoming almost fae. Who knows where the species is headed? Personally, I think the warpers feel threatened. We're not so special anymore."

I grunted. "Special enough, if The Flare didn't affect you all. What about your friends? Where are they?"

"I told you before, they weren't really my friends. Turns out, that boyfriend of my cousin's was a warper, and his friends, too. Apparently, I was making too much of a fuss about my cousin's disappearance, not letting it go, and they decided this was an easy way to bring me in for conversion. The worst part? One of the women back in those cells says Clarice and Tom were here. She says he brought Clarice in, against her will, but my cousin converted quickly, in days. Usually, it takes weeks to really convert someone deep down, not just mind warp them with some thought control. She didn't even resist. Tom had her completely fooled. They all did." He shook his head in disgust.

"I guess, if she loved him?"

"Please. Warpers are so twisted, there's no real love in their hearts. No. I don't know. She's not who I thought she was, that's all."

"I'm sorry."

"Not your fault. Come on. We should get running again."

He started jogging, and I matched his pace.

"So, what's your power, then?"

"Astral travel. My consciousness can leave my body, visit other places, other people's dreams, that kind of thing."

"Seriously? That is so cool. So, were you able to tell anyone where you were? Can you get help, call in reinforcements?"

He shook his head no.

"They kept us all doped up on something, it blocks our powers while they are converting us. It takes at least a day to wear off."

"Well, that sucks. I guess we just have to keep going then. My brother will find us, eventually."

"How?"

"Earth powers, remember? He can connect to the trees, or if we're lucky he's already had a vision. He'll find us."

"I hope you're right."

I grimaced.

"Me, too."

Chapter 20

We ran. We walked. We talked some more. David told me how his people tried to raise their children carefully, always making sure they understood the risks of power and abuse. Like the fae, starseeds weren't born with abilities. Unlike us, they didn't get their powers until they were at least twenty-eight, sometimes later. Something about the effect of Saturn's orbit on their DNA, and lunar and solar eclipses all acting as triggers for their abilities.

Abilities traveled in families, and were considered lunar or solar, depending on whether they had more active or passive effects. Some abilities tended to increase the chances of the warping, the seduction to power: mind control; telekinesis; the production of holograms or glamours. Those three solar powers offered more opportunity for corruption, since they could be abused so much more easily for personal gain.

Though, of course, anyone could become a warper after their powers woke up.

My mom was going to be so annoyed to find out that not everyone had been affected by The Flare. All that hard work, everything she had gone through, and for what. True evil still lurked under the veneer of civilization.

It was a sobering, disturbing realization.

Nothing would ever feel the same again. How many humans had I already met who were not what they seemed?

David said probably none, that there really weren't that many of them. I felt skeptical. Seemed to me like there had to be a fair amount, after that many centuries of dissemination throughout the world gene pool. Then again, math had never really been my thing.

I was puzzling it out, running several feet ahead of David when a tree exploded behind me. I heard the blast, and a crack, and whirled to see sparks falling to the ground. David just missed being hit by a limb as it crashed to the ground. I'd thought the storm was ending, but apparently, I was wrong.

David's eyes widened, and he increased his pace, narrowing the gap between us. A wise idea, if more lightning was on the way. I focused on the ground in front of me and picked up speed.

Then, I heard a shout, and David screamed behind me. I looked over my shoulder and stopped in my tracks, shocked to see vines whipping off a tree and wrapping themselves around my friend, yanking him up into the canopy of leaves above my head.

"David!" I yelled.

This wasn't the storm, or warpers. This was fae.

I spun in place, and came face to face with Hollis. "Hollis!" Overcome with relief, I hugged my brother tightly. His arms came around me, but they felt like angry bands of steel, rigid and hard.

"Are you okay?"

"Yes, I'm fine, I-"

And then his arms relaxed, and I was sinking into a full on bear hug, the air being squeezed out of me.

Behind me, David screamed again, this time in pain. I looked up, and saw shocks of blue and white sparking along his body.

"Khai!" I screamed at my friend, who paused, mid-tase. "What the hell are you doing?"

The look on his face was one of pure rage, but it slowly melted as he looked at me. He rushed over, and Hollis released me. Khai grabbed me by the shoulders and inspected my face, my body.

"Did he hurt you?"

"Did he-? No. Of course not. Guys, you have to let him down. David didn't do anything."

Hollis shook his head to the contrary. "He was chasing you. Look at you, you're covered in mud. What happened?"

"Nothing happened," David shouted. "Ana, tell them."

I bit my lip. The sooner we got David safely out of the woods, the better, but the last thing I wanted was for the guys to call off our trip because of some weirdos in the woods. Something like this, Khai and Hollis would be treating me like I was even more fragile than before. No. I wasn't ready for that. If I had to, I would tell them, but not yet. If we could get back to our site, and make trail, I had a feeling we'd be okay. We just needed to keep moving. The warpers would be looking for David, not me. Starseeds, not a bunch of fae kids.

"Yeah, we just... Well, after I stormed off, I got lost. Luckily, I ran into David here, who hurt his ankle. He's um, been separated from his friends for days, lost his pack and everything. I healed him, and then the storm hit, and we had to take shelter. Once the lightning calmed down a bit, we decided to try and find you guys – Hollis, I knew you would find me eventually. David wasn't chasing me, we were just trail-running." I looked up at David, eyes willing him to go along with my story.

"Really? You looked pretty freaked out, Ana," Hollis said doubtfully.

"Well, yeah, some freak lightning almost killed us back there, so yeah, I was pretty scared," I said, glaring at Khai.

"Sorry about that," Khai said, looking chagrined.

Hollis sighed, and made a gesture of release with his hands. The vines holding David aloft slowly began to untwine, lowering him gently to the ground. Well, mostly gently. The last few feet were more of a drop, and he landed squarely on his feet with a thud.

"Now you see what I mean about active powers?" I asked him.

"Yeah, I see." David rubbed his chest where Khai had hit him.

"Sorry, man," Khai said, manning up.

"It's okay. I would have done the same thing in your shoes, I think."

"Right, well, now that that's all settled... How about we get back to camp? We still have a couple of hours of daylight left, and I think we should go to town so David can get new gear and stuff. Plus, he should still probably have that ankle looked at, just to be safe."

"Yeah, okay. We can figure it out at camp. Come on, we're actually pretty close. Jules is worried sick, too," Hollis said, concern crossing his face again.

"Here's your watch." Khai handed me the GPS bracelet. "I'm really sorry about earlier, I didn't mean what I said, at least, not the way you think I-"

"Let's not talk about it now, okay?" I put up a hand stopping him. "Let's just get back to camp."

"Okay. Hold on." He reached up and wiped a smear of dirt from under my eye. "Gods, you're a mess."

"I know," I grinned ruefully. "So much for my bath."

His blue eyes darkened, and he didn't return my smile. Instead, he brushed more dirt from myhair, and then swallowed.

"I really am sorry. I don't know why I can't seem to stop worrying about you. But I do."

"It's okay, Khai." I thought of where David and I had come from, and how right Khai would have been to worry. And then, I imagined his reaction if he knew what I'd discovered. How much more over-protective he and Hollis would become then. Just the idea of it strengthened my resolve to keep it to myself. Not forever. Just for a few days. Or maybe until Montreal. Or maybe until I got married. I don't know.

Right now, I just wanted to get out of this part of the woods, get clean again, and get David to safety.

"Come on, let's go."

I took his hand and tugged, leading the way for a moment until I realized I didn't know where I was going. I released Khai, and let him take point. David jogged up to me and walked beside me in silence, Hollis bringing up the rear.

"You sure this is how you want to play it?" David whispered.

"Yeah. You saw how they are. This is for the best, trust me."

He nodded, and sighed, rubbing his chest again.

"You okay?" I asked.

"Yeah, just stings a bit. Your friend Sparky really packs a wallop."

"Yeah. He's been practicing."

"Lucky me."

"At least he didn't kill you."

"There is that."

"So, what do you think? Can you make it home from town?" I asked.

"I don't know. I mean, they'll be looking for me. They know who I am, where I live. I can't go home." I could practically feel the fear rolling off him as he spoke. "If you don't mind, I think it might be safer to stay with you guys, head to the local headquarters for my people in Montreal. If you guys don't mind? I mean, I can totally hike on by myself, it's just that you guys-"

I laid my hand on his arm. "Please. Don't say another word. I get it. I'd want to walk with us, too. Of course you can."

"Thanks, Ana. That really means a lot. You've already done so much for me. If it wasn't for you-"

"Shh. Don't say it. We're okay. Everything is going to be okay."

He reached over and laid his hand upon mind on his arm, and gave it a small squeeze.

"Thanks."

I smiled at him, our eyes meeting warmly. We were worlds apart, in years, and apparently even DNA, but at that moment, I felt closer to David than anyone I'd ever known. Overwhelmed by the emotion I felt returned in his gaze, I looked away, removing my hand from his arm.

We kept moving, allowing an awkward silence to settle over us. The rain had stopped, and the mud and wet clothes were beginning to weigh heavily on my body. I couldn't wait to get back to camp.

Thankfully, I didn't have to walk long. In less than ten minutes, we were rounding the corner of the stone walls of the barn, coming face to face with Jules. For a moment, I imagined what might have happened if the warpers had stumbled across her by herself. Then I erased the thought from my head. They were looking for starseeds, not lone girls in the woods.

The knowledge that the warpers might have other uses for a defenseless human, a race they seemed less than keen on, was something I didn't really want to think about as my friend locked her long, muscled arms around me.

"Ana! I was so worried about you. That storm was insane! You look a mess, girl." She fussed over me, trying to clean me up a bit, and I let her try, even though anyone could see it was a lost cause. "And David? How did you two end up together?"

I quickly told her what I told Hollis, and she clucked her tongue, as if it all made sense. As if it was along the lines of what she'd already imagined. Because, really, who would have imagined the truth? Who would ever think a group of empowered alien hybrids had set up a torture camp in the woods for converting soldiers to their twisted cause of world domination?

Am I right?

Which I suppose is why they'd done it here, in the first place. And why we needed to move. Quickly.

"So, um, I'm just going to clean up a bit in the stream, and then I think we should head to town. I've been looking on my GPS and it's only a couple miles south through the woods there. David needs to get looked at by a doctor."

"Yeah, okay, no problem." Jules looked over to where Khai and Hollis had already started to break down our camp, and David was folding up a ground tarp. "You sure there isn't anything else you want to tell me?"

"No, what do you mean?" I asked, trying to look innocent.

"Like, why you ran off in the first place? Khai was all kinds of upset when he came back. What's going on with you two?"

The question came out of left field, and I wasn't sure how to catch it.

"I, I don't know," I stammered. "He keeps talking to me like I'm some sort of fragile flower that needs protecting. It's getting on my nerves."

"Okay." She chewed her lip, eyeing me curiously. "If that's all."

"Trust me. You've never had anyone treat you like this. I mean, look at you. You're tall, gorgeous, athletic. Everyone knows you can take care of yourself. You- What?"

I broke off as Jules started cracking up.

"Oh my God. You! Girl, I am a young black woman. You think hundreds of years of stereotypes and discrimination have entirely melted away? I mean, sure, The Flare has really improved things, yeah, but people still treat me like I'm not up to their level sometimes. Just because I'm a girl, or black. And my daddy isn't any different than yours. He'd lock me up in a tower to keep me safe, if he thought he could get away with it. But with our dads, and guys like your brother and Khai, I don't think they're underestimating us. I think they just care too much."

"Mmm. I guess. It's still annoying."

"It's better than the alternative, though, right?"

"What's that?"

"Them not caring."

"Oh. I guess you're right. I hadn't thought of it that way." I watched Khai, and could feel any residual anger I had slipping away. I never could stay mad at anyone for long. David dropped a tent pole, the clatter drawing my attention and we locked eyes, sharing a smile even as he bent to pick it up.

"Oh, and what's this?" Jules cooed, hip checking me.

"What?"

"You and David? Was this really a chance meeting in the woods, or was it planned?"

"Planned?" I asked, confused by her line of thinking.

"You know, a secret rendezvous with a handsome, older man? Eh?" She waggled her eyebrows and I blushed.

"No!" I said loudly, attracting the guys' attention. I leaned in towards Jules. "No," I said more quietly. It was not planned. There's nothing going on. I mean he's nice, but-"

"Okay, okay, you don't have to say anymore. I know you are hiding something, but that's okay. My lips are sealed." She winked, and pretended to lock a key over her closed mouth. I rolled my eyes.

"Whatever. I'm going to clean up." I grabbed a clean shirt and walked behind the shelter towards a small stream. Once my face and arms were washed, I pulled off my once yellow, now brown-stained top and put on a clean raspberry-colored tank top. Examining the yellowish shirt, I sighed. I doubted it would ever be clean again, but at least I could try. I rinsed it several times in the stream, squeezed out the excess water and walked back to my pack where I stowed it away with my other dirty laundry. Maybe there would be a laundromat in town.

Chapter 21

On the way to town, I talked to Hollis about David continuing on with us, at least for a while.

"Well, sure, of course, if he wants to continue on. Sounds to me like those friends of his aren't such great pals if they left him."

Hollis had no idea.

"I said the same thing." Not a lie. "They were friends of his cousin's boyfriend, he barely knows them." Again, not a lie.

"So what's his plan? He still looking for his cousin?"

"Um, I don't know. I think he's sort of come to terms with her being gone. I think he just wants to finish the trail now. You know. Complete something." Maybe just the smallest stretch of the truth.

"Makes sense. Thru-hikes are known for being cathartic," Hollis said sagely.

"Right. Yeah, cathartic. He said he has some relatives in Montreal, so I think he might go all the way with us, stay with them for a while."

"That's cool. It'll be nice to have some more testosterone on this trip." He winked, and I rolled my eyes.

"Really? I don't know, I think we've got a bit more than we need," I said, waving a hand over him.

Hollis laughed, and shouted ahead to David. "Hey, Mud! Ana says you'd like to hike with us all the way to Montreal. Welcome to the team!"

"Mud?" I laughed.

"Thanks, Hollis," David yelled, walking backwards and giving us two thumbs up.

"Oh, Hollis has a trail name, now. Call him Mr. Perfect," I called out.

"Okay." David grinned. "Thanks, Mr. Perfect."

"Anytime, Mud!"

"Aw, crap. Is that my trail name, now?"

"Have you seen yourself?" I laughed.

"Right," David – Mud – drawled. He gave me a little mock salute and turned back around to face the trail.

"I like him," Hollis said with approval.

"Me, too," I mused.

We hiked on, and finally came to a road crossing.

"Route 125," Khai said, looking at a map. "Middlebury isn't that far, it should have all the gear David needs. We just need to hitch a ride."

Jules looked over our grubby group. "For five of us?"

"A pick-up will do the trick. We'll find one." Hollis reassured her.

In the end, it was a minivan that picked us up. The woman driving was clearly the mother of quite a few kids, judging by the spilled food and toys all over the back seats. She apologized for the mess, and I quickly pointed out our own lack of hygiene. Eyeing David, she chuckled, and handed him a worn beach towel to sit on.

"I always keep one on hand for emergencies. You just never know," she sighed.

Indeed. You really never did.

Meggie, as she introduced herself, was able to drop us off just a couple blocks away from The Outdoor Superstore. Which was perfect, really, because we were able to buy fresh fish tacos and sodas from a food truck parked along the way.

Walking with David, I hoped I wasn't moaning or humming too much while I ate. I still couldn't believe that was something I did. Worse, how was I supposed to stop if I didn't even realize I was doing it?

Ugh.

Life could be so embarrassing sometimes.

But, given the alternative – not eating these amazing tacos – I could live with it.

Taking the last bite, I looked over at David. He was smiling at me, like I'd done something really cute or funny.

Oh gods. I must have been humming.

I smiled back, cleared my throat and smiled. "So, um, I wanted to thank you again for not saying anything to my friends about the whole starseed thing. Khai and Hollis, they're so overprotective. I don't want them to call off the trip. I know, it's silly. Probably totally insane, considering how dangerous the warpers are. I mean, they're still out there. But I've been looking forward to this trip for practically forever, you know?"

"I know what you mean. When I started out, all I cared about was finding Clarise. But the more I hiked, the more the woods grew on me. I love being on the trail." He paused, looking down at the taco in his hand. "They took her away from me. Away from my family. I'm not going to let them take away this, too. I want to finish this, see the whole trail. See Montreal."

"You will," I said, reaching out and squeezing his arm.

"Thanks to you." He looked up, and dazzled me with the full force of his smile. "I've never met anyone like you before."

"No fae at all?"

"Fae? No, I've met fae. I mean, you're different. What you did back there at the camp, freeing everyone, healing me. You never faltered, not for a second. I spent the whole time I was there going between being angry and being terrified. But you – you were so calm. So fearless. You're amazing."

I didn't know what to say. I certainly hadn't felt calm, and no one had ever really said anything like that to me before. I mean, maybe my parents, or Jules. But no one else. To everyone who knew me, I'd always just been Ana, Hollis' quiet little sister.

I felt like I'd been seen, really seen, for the first time in my life.

And it felt amazing.

I realized David was gazing at me, and I still hadn't said a word. "Thank you," I said, and blushed.

"Don't thank me," he said, taking my hand in his. "I should be thanking you, every hour. I was supposed to start conversion therapy tomorrow morning. If you'd arrived a few days later, who knows who, or what I would have become. I owe you more than my life. I owe you myself."

"Are you going to pledge a life debt to me now, offer me a year of service?" I teased.

"I'm sorry, what?"

"Nothing, never mind. It's a story my mom told me all the time when I was little, how she once saved the life of this little squirrel, and he pledged his life to hers for a year." I giggled, feeling silly.

"Well if a squirrel can do it, I can, too. In a heartbeat. I would do anything for you, Ana. Not just for a year, for the rest of my life."

"Whoa. Easy there." He sounded so serious, so earnest. I appreciated his gratitude, but I didn't need it. "Don't be so eager to pledge yourself. My mom's squirrel died saving her life."

"Hopefully we've seen the last of the Warpers, and it will never come to that. But I mean it, Ana. I owe you everything I am. You saved me from getting warped. It's not a small thing."

"Okay. Okay. Well, let's keep it quiet, alright?" We'd arrived at the Superstore.

"Whatever you need," he said with a sly grin. I rolled my eyes and dragged him towards the double doors.

A whole world of gear and insta-food was waiting within, and I had a man by the hand who needed outfitting.

"No, Mud. Whatever you need."

Chapter 22

David got everything he needed in town, thanks to some helpful salespeople and a special credit account my Dad had set up for Hollis and I, good at any Outdoor Superstore nationwide, in case the need arose. I wasn't one hundred percent sure that Dad would consider outfitting a stranger a real "need" but I'd worry about that later. Lucky for David, he had his own hiking boots and wouldn't have to worry about breaking them in on the trail. For a thru-hiker, even the smallest blisters were a danger best avoided.

One hour of shopping, a night in a motel, and we were back on the trail the next morning. The weather was gorgeous again, not a cloud in the sky. No sign of the rain from the day before.

David walked with me most of the time. It was nice getting to know someone new, someone I hadn't spent over a decade in school with. Not that I would ever have been in school with David – at one point in our sharing David admitted he was twenty-eight. His astral abilities had just been awakened six months earlier, a couple months after his birthday. I'd felt a little awkward then, knowing he was so much older than me. Almost a decade.

Not that it mattered, really. I mean, once we got to Montreal I'd probably never see him again.

So what if I was starting to think I might want to?

Anyway, it couldn't matter, like I said.

Who cared that he was funny, and kind, and honest?

Right. Well. I turned my mind away from any thoughts like that, and just tried to enjoy the walk.

If we both jumped every time we heard a squirrel, or passed a group of unknown hikers, well, it was to be expected. The Warpers were out there, somewhere. They could still be looking for David. For us. Anyone could be a warper. No one was safe. Not anymore.

The sanctity of the trail had been broken.

It helped when Jules walked with us for a while, and that night David crashed early in his tent. No wonder, either. He must have been exhausted after everything he'd been through, and I could tell that his nerves were still taking a toll. It didn't make me think any less of him. If I were him, I imagined I would have slept for days.

The next day, Khai stuck by my side, so there wasn't any opportunity for me to find out more about starseeds. With Khai around, conversation was stilted. The two guys just didn't seem to get along, though they both tried. I could tell Khai still didn't quite trust David. The way he looked at him every time he spoke, like a puzzle he couldn't quite figure out? Yeah, clear giveaway.

I gave Khai the eye a few times, trying to tell him to knock it off, but each time I felt like a fraud.

Khai was right. David had lied to him. We had lied to all of them. The guilt weighed on me, but not as much as the need to try and make it through the rest of the trip in one, happy, trail-worn-and-fulfilled piece.

Even worse were the few times that David and I would laugh together, and Khai's left eyebrow would lower in displeasure, or he would say something rude just to ruin the moment. As if I couldn't have another friend, other than him, Khai. I swear, he was almost as infuriating as Hollis sometimes.

When we finally made camp that evening, it was a relief. We arrived at the three-sided log shelter named after Theron Dean, one of the original founding members of the Long Trail. The shelter had been rebuilt several times. Now, it could accommodate six or seven people comfortably on its interior raised sleeping platform. The platform was no longer made of hard wood, but fashioned from a durable, weather-proof natural synthetic that had the same sort of give to it as a thick bed of moss. It was amazing, and it was something that the tech gurus of Valhalla had created a couple decades ago, after teaming up with a team of Japanese polymer specialists. Together, the humans and fae had created GrounSoft, which was now used to make a huge range of things, from bus seats to bathroom floors.

It was the first time I'd encountered it on the trail, and I wasn't sorry for it. Laying down on my sleeping bag, it was as good as being in a real bed. I sighed, content to relax for a while. Hollis and Jules were cooking dinner; Khai and David had gone off to collect more water and firewood. My job, setting up the shelter for later, was the easiest. I'd already taken out all the supplies we'd need that night – lanterns, bowls, utensils – and hung up our packs on the provided nails.

Time for a rest.

I listened to the birds singing their last songs of the evening, the quiet hush of Jules' voice, the low rumble of Hollis' answer. Giggles. More talking.

All was well with the world. I smiled, and closed my eyes, and drifted off to sleep.

I dreamt of the forest. I dreamt of smiles. I dreamt of passion and longing.

And then I woke up. An intense sadness gripped me, one that I could not reconcile with the heat of the dreams I'd been having.

That's when I heard it. The crying.

"Jules?" The word came out in a sleepy mumble, my body not quite caught up with my brain. I sat up and shook my head, trying to clear it. "Jules!"

I climbed down from the platform and hopped off the shelter. Hollis was standing a few feet away from my friend, hands in his pockets, watching her cry with a strange look on his face. Dismay, mixed with resolve and regret. It was a look I'd never seen on his face before.

"What happened? Jules?" I rushed to her side where she was sitting on the hard-packed earth, pulling her to me. "Hollis?"

"I-" The resolve hardened on his face and he shook his head. "I can't."

And then, he turned on his heel and walked away, into the woods.

Jules began sobbing then, and I looked her in the face. "Jules, talk to me. What's going on? Take a breath and tell me, please."

"He," she hiccupped, "he kissed me."

"You guys have been hanging out all the time. Isn't this what you wanted? Was it bad?"

"It is." She wiped her eyes, and took a deep breath. "And it was great. It was amazing. I mean, it wasn't just a kiss. It was like... I don't know, I mean we were just laughing and teasing each other and then his eyes kind of went all silvery and he just said 'screw it', and started kissing me like he'd never stop."

"But that's great, Jules!" The fact that we were talking about my brother didn't even skeeve me out that much, I was so happy for my friend.

"Yeah. It was. Until he did stop."

My smile fell, then, because I knew what she was going to say.

"Somehow I'd ended up in his lap, and it was just amazing, everything I'd ever imagined, and then all of a sudden I was back on the ground, and he was standing, there." She pointed to where Hollis had been moments before.

Her eyes narrowed, remembering.

"He said-" she released an angry groan and took a deep breath. "He said that he was really sorry, that he didn't know what he'd been thinking. I said it was okay, that we were both adults. And then his face just kind of changed, and he said that he didn't feel *that* way about me, and that he'd just been on the trail too long. And *then* he actually had the gall to joke that he'd been too long without a woman and he laughed."

"He. Did. Not."

"He did. I couldn't believe it. I figured he was just embarrassed, since I'm your friend. I thought if I opened up a little, he would, too. So I told him."

"Told him what?" I asked, eyeing her. Hoping she hadn't.

"I told him it was okay. That I liked him. That I'd always liked him."

Yep. She had.

"Oh, Jules."

"I know!" she wailed, and started crying again.

"It's going to be okay. Okay? Don't worry. He'll come around." I wasn't sure that was true, but right now, I knew what she needed to hear.

"I made such a fool of myself. He just stood there, looking at me, shaking his head. That's when I started crying. Jesus, Ana, how can my heart feel so broken, when it didn't even get a chance to be in love?"

"Oh, Jules. I don't know. I'm so sorry. Why don't you go lie down, get some rest? I'll bring you something to eat later, okay?"

"Okay," she sniffled. She gave me a long hug, so desperate that my own heart started to crack, and then she withdrew. "Thanks, Ana."

I smiled and nodded, and watched her as she retreated to the safety of her sleeping bag. Now I was really glad that I had put hers against the wall, next to mine, where no one else could bother her.

With suspiciously good timing, David and Khai walked quietly back into the clearing.

"Hey guys," I said.

"Hey," they answered.

David dropped his bundle of wood on top of Khai's and sat down across from me. "Everything okay?"

"Yeah, why?" I asked.

Khai looked at me with concern. "We heard crying. We didn't want to bother you guys so..."

"We waited," David finished.

"Oh. Right. Well, Jules and Hollis had a bit of a... fight. Hollis said something mean to Jules, and she's pretty tired so she got more upset than she meant to. Anyhow, nothing big."

It wasn't my place to spread the word about what had happened. If Hollis wanted to tell Khai, he could, but for now I would keep it to myself.

Unfortunately, Khai was a bit too astute for that.

"He made her cry? Like, in a Mad River kind of way, cry?" He looked concerned, I'll give him that, but the small quirk to his upper lip made me want to punch him.

"This isn't the time, Khai," I huffed.

"What's Mad River?" David asked innocently.

"Oh, nothing. Just a little bet Ana and I have going on." Khai smirked at David, before turning back to me. "You do know that we'll hit the Glen tomorrow before lunch, right?"

I hadn't known that, but I didn't care. "So? I can't believe you're sitting there grinning. She's crying, Khai. Crying. You're a terrible friend, you know that?"

His face fell, and came to my side, putting a hand on my arm. "Hey, I'm sorry, okay. I didn't know it was that serious."

"Well, it is, okay? Or it was. I don't know." I stirred the pot on the fire. "Can we not talk about it now? Hollis could come back any second."

"Sure, no problem. I am sorry, really, okay?"

"Yeah, whatever. Fine. Can you stir this? I'm gonna go check on Jules."

I peeked in on my friend, careful not to disturb her. She was curled in a ball on her side, facing the wall, eyes closed, breathing deeply as she slept. I was glad she wasn't still crying, glad she'd found some respite.

When Hollis finally returned, he wouldn't look at me. To Khai, he announced he was going to sleep outside, then he grabbed his dinner and his sleeping bag, and retreated to the low, private shelter of a weeping pine.

No jokes. No superiority.

It wasn't the Hollis I knew.

Which was gratifying, in a way. It meant that the kiss had affected him, somehow, or at least he was upset he'd hurt Jules. Either way, it was always nice to know Hollis had actual feelings.

Chapter 23

He was a heartless, arrogant pig. No, scratch that. A heartless, gutless, arrogant miscreant. Pigs were cute.

Hollis was not.

He hadn't looked at Jules, spoken to her or smiled at anyone yet this morning.

Jules, meanwhile, had looked only at the ground. It was like she'd lost a piece of herself. The part that made her shine.

I'd stuck with Jules on the trail all day so far, glaring at the backs of the men, who all walked ahead, Hollis on his own and Khai following with David, while Jules continued to look down.

We followed the ridge of Mount Ellen to Stark Mountain, stopping to eat and rest at Stark's Nest, a gorgeous modern building complete with a wraparound deck overlooking the Mad River Glen ski resort. During the summer, the resort left the "warming hut" open to thru-hikers, allowing them to stay there overnight as needed. Of course, it wasn't really a hut anymore. It had been expanded over the years, so that now it was pretty fabulous, boasting multiple couches, board games, tables and chairs. It even had a bathroom and three bunk rooms. The best part? A small solar shower outside that I aimed to claim before we left.

Everyone was eating, each in their own little spot. I'd chosen a patch of grass in the sun. The far infrared rays of the sun loosened my muscles, the gentle heat penetrating deep inside me, relaxing me. Or, maybe it was just that I wasn't near my friends. I loved Jules, and my brother, but the tension between them was a drain on my soul, weighing me down. I put my granola to the side and laid down, arms open wide. Like a sacrifice, I offered myself to the sun.

Asked for cleansing. For clarity. For a happier day.

Instead, darkness fell.

Oh, okay, maybe nothing so dramatic. But a shadow did fall across my body, blocking the heat of the sun, and I opened my eyes.

Khai stood above me, dark in shadow against the golden aura of our central star.

"What do you want?"

"Nice to see you, too."

I sat up. "Uh-huh. So?"

"So, I know you think I was insensitive last night, and I don't want you to get mad at me, but I'm here to collect."

"Collect what?" I sneered.

"On our bet."

"Are you serious?"

"Well, yeah. We bet, you lost. Jules, in tears, by Mad River. That was the deal. So now, winner gets ruling rights."

"You've got to be kidding me. This is so not the time-"

"Hey, look, you're the one who termed the wager."

"I don't mean that," I said, climbing to my feet. "I mean, don't you think that Jules might be upset to have a bet rubbed in her face right now?"

"Oh, that," Khai waved his hand. Don't worry. No one needs to know. I only have one thing I want you to do."

"One thing?" I asked, puzzled. Staring up into his dark face, the sun still behind him, I couldn't see much of his expression. Only his clear, bright blue eyes, staring down into mine.

"Yes. One thing," he said in a low voice.

For a second, my heart skipped, a strange, stuttering beat. I didn't know what he was about to ask, but suddenly I was a bundle of nerves.

"I want you to ditch David."

"I'm sorry, what?" I'd heard the words, but they didn't make sense.

"I want you to tell David that he has to hike on his own. Or go into town. Go home. Whatever. But he can't hike with us, not anymore."

"I can't do that," I protested.

"Ruling rights say you can, and you will."

"I will not." I narrowed my eyes at him, putting my hands on my hips. "What's your problem with him, anyway?"

"I don't know," he said, "he seems like a nice guy-"

"He is."

"But something's off," Khai finished. "Something's not right about him, Ana, can't you tell? He's lying about something. I've tried asking him questions, and he just brushes me off. He's barely tried to find his friends. He

154

sticks to you like glue. I mean, he's what, 30? He's too old to be following you around like that."

"He's twenty-eight, and what do you mean, "like that'? He's not a pedophile, it's not like I'm a kid or something."

"You might as well be, to him. What kind of grown man follows a 19-year-old girl around?"

I crossed my arms, glaring at him.

"Okay, that came out wrong. But come on. You really can't tell he's not telling us the whole truth?"

"Look, David is a good guy. I trust him. And I am not going to leave him out here alone on the trail."

"Fine. We'll drop him off at the next town."

"No."

"Dammit, Ana!" he shouted in frustration, his anger palpable. That was okay. I had enough of my own.

"No!" I yelled back, shoving him away from me at the same time.

I just meant to push him back a little. Vent some of my annoyance.

I never meant what happened next.

I never meant for him to hit the ground so hard.

Everything I was feeling, everything I was upset about, came out of me with a wail when I touched him. It was like a wave of something cold and blue exploded from my hands, pushing him away from me in a burst even before my hands made contact.

"Oh my gods, Khai!" I rushed forward, cradling his head. I took his pulse, which was steady. But he didn't open his eyes.

"Ana?" Hollis came running around the ski lift, finding us on the grass. "What happened? I heard you guys yelling, and I thought I saw a flash."

"We were arguing, and then- I don't know. I don't know what happened."

"Did he tase himself? You know, I told him-"

"No. I don't think so. I think I did this."

"How?" Hollis looked at me, intrigued.

"I told you, I don't know. I was mad, and I wanted to push him away, and then-"

Khai started coughing, and I brushed his hair back. "Shh. You're okay. It's okay."

And then he started laughing.

"Oh gods. I broke him." He was obviously concussed. "Khai, do you know where you are?"

Hollis pointed two fingers at the sky. "Khai, how many fingers am I holding up?"

Laughing even harder, Khai waved him away, sitting up.

"I'm fine, really. Stop it, you two. Oh gods, I can't breathe," he said, putting a hand to his chest before collapsing in laughter again.

"Khai!" Hollis said sharply. "What happened? What's so funny?"

"You are. She is. Don't you get what's going on?"

"No, Khai," I said, exasperated. "Why don't you tell us?"

Khai looked at me, bemused, a crooked smile on his face.

"Ana's a water fae."

Chapter 24

"I'm a what?"

"A water fae."

"I am not."

"You are. Trust me. I felt it. That was no flash that hit me. Those were pure emotions. Knocked me on my ass, too."

"But I can't be. Can I?" I looked at Hollis for confirmation.

"I don't know," he mused. "Mom and Dad are both earth fae, sure, but not everyone in our family is. Yvain is a water fae, for one."

Yvain Le Fay, the father of our grandfather, Bran.

"But-" The protest died on my lips, Khai and Hollis both watching me. And it started to come back to me, the way it had rained more when I was sad. The thunderstorm when Khai and I had fought before. The emotional roller coaster I'd been on lately. "Oh no."

"Oh, yes." Khai whooped, hugging me. "Don't you see? You've finally got those active powers you've been wanting so badly."

"But... Water? I hardly know anything about that element. I always assumed..."

"Don't worry, sis. We'll help you figure it out. We'll line up a teacher for you when we get to Montreal. You'll figure it out."

Looking at me, Khai's eyebrow lowered.

"What?" I asked. "I thought you were happy for me."

"I am," he said, looking over my shoulder. I turned, and saw David approaching with Jules.

"Everything okay?" he asked, concerned.

"No. No, it's not." Khai stood, facing David.

"Oh, what's wrong?" David asked, his gaze bouncing between Khai and I.

"You need to leave," Khai stated in a firm voice.

"What?" Jules exclaimed. "Khai, you can't just be rude like that."

"He does not have to leave," I growled, standing, too.

"Khai?" Hollis asked patiently. "What's going on?"

"This guy," he said, jabbing a finger at David, "has been lying to us.

David looked at me, but didn't say anything.

"Don't you look at her," Khai sneered. "You look at me. That's right. I know something's up. I don't know what you're hiding, and I don't really care. It doesn't matter to me, because you're going to go your own way now. Got it?"

"No, he's not," I said grimly.

"He is."

"Um, Khai? How about we all sit down and talk about this?" Hollis said in an easy voice, his debate team voice, the one that always won over all the judges.

"No!" Khai and I both yelled at the same time. Khai looked at me, surprised.

"Ana-"

"Screw your ruling rights, Khai, and screw you. We're out of here. Come on, David." I grabbed his hand and pulled him away, marching back towards Stark's Nest.

"Ana, where are we going?" David said, pulling his hand from mine as we walked.

"We're leaving. I'm not going to send you off on your own. And Khai doesn't deserve to know anything more than that. I'm *done*." As if for emphasis, a flash of lightning lit across the clear blue sky, and thunder rumbled high in the atmosphere.

I took a deep breath, reaching for calm. If I really was making the rain and thunder, then I needed to relax. The last thing I wanted right now was a deluge.

"I'm done," I said more calmly. Steps pounded behind me and turned warily, only to see Jules.

"Wait up!"

"I'm not staying, Jules. You heard him. I've had it with his attitude. David and I will meet you guys in Montreal."

"You think I want to walk with those losers by myself?" she scoffed. "No way. I'm coming with you guys."

"Really?" I lit up with a grin.

"Of course!"

"All right, then. Let's hurry before those two realize we're serious."

David shook his head, looking worried. "You sure you guys want to do this? I don't want to cause any trouble."

"Oh please," Jules said. "You've been nothing but a perfect gentleman. It's those two, they think they're god's gift. You have no idea."

I bit back another grin, thinking about how much her tune had changed in the last twenty-four hours. Leave it to my brother, and his love 'em and leave 'em attitude. There was a reason he didn't have any female friends.

"Alright, if you're both sure."

We'd arrived at the Nest. Jules and I looked at each other. As we had so many times before, we spoke as one, best-friend brains in sync. "We're sure."

Packs on, we were just hitting the trail when Hollis jogged up to us.

"Ana, wait! You can't leave."

"You bet your damn holy butt I can," I retorted.

"Ana. Please. What about Dad and Mom?"

"What about them? I'll call them at the next town. But I'm not changing my mind."

"Jules? Can't you change her mind?"

"Change her mind? Are you kidding? I'm going with her." She stood tall and strong, and sounded tough, but I could see it in her eyes. She was imploring him to ask her to stay.

And he totally missed it. Gods, he could be such an idiot.

"Fine. Have it your way. Here, Jules, take your chats, at least." He tossed her the small box from his pack, watching her unlock it with the key from around her neck. Once she'd removed our chats, he took the box back from her and nodded.

"Okay, well, call us if you need us, at least?"

"Okay," I agreed.

"Fine. I guess that's it, then. We'll see you both in Montreal." He dismissed us with a look and turned to David.

"I trust you, even if Khai doesn't. If anything happens to either of these girls, I will track you down, and I will make you regret you ever lived. Got it?"

"Got it." David nodded solemnly. "Don't worry about them. We'll be okay."

"Good. We'll only be a day behind you. You hear that, little sister? One day. I'm giving you that. You change your mind, you wait for us, and we'll be there soon enough."

"Gee, what a gift," Jules muttered, and I laughed.

"Sorry." I tried to look serious, and failed. "Oh cheer up Hollis. We made it this far together. Now you and Khai can have some bromance time to yourselves." I stepped up to him and gave him a hug. "See you on the flip side."

"You better," he murmured, and kissed the top of my head.

Jules shuffled her feet noisily at my side, and I let him go. It was time.

Chapter 25

"Well," Jules huffed, walking next to me. "Now that we're away from the drama, care to enlighten me about exactly what just happened?"

"What? Oh, sure. Yes." I looked behind me. David was several yards behind us, and I gave him a small smile before turning back to Jules.

"Khai said David's been lying to us. I trust you, Ana, you know I do, but what is going on, really? The looks you two keep giving each other, it's not just because you have the hots for him. It's more than that."

"I do not have-"

She raised an eyebrow and I changed tack.

"Never mind. You're right. There is more to what happened with David and his friends than what we told you all. But before we get to that, I should probably come clean about something else."

"Okay," Jules said, looking at me oddly.

I'd never lied to Jules before, not that I could remember. And now I had multiple explanations to make. This wasn't going to be easy. Best to get it over with quickly.

"Khai and I had a bet going about you and Hollis." I said the words in a rush, and then I cringed, waiting for her reaction.

"You...with Khai?"

I nodded.

"Did you at least bet in my favor?"

"Of course! Khai was all, 'there's no way this will end well, Hollis is a dog,' and I said he was underestimating you, and that you'd have Hollis eating out of your hand soon enough."

"Really, you said that?"

"Well, yeah! Khai bet that you'd be heartbroken by Mad River Glen. I was so annoyed, I agreed to his terms, ruler's rights for a day."

"No way, ruler's rights? I can't remember the last time we played that."

"I know. Me, neither. Anyway, today we got to Mad River, and he said he had only one demand – that David had to go. I got so mad, he's been making me so crazy lately, I just kind of snapped. And then my power activated, and the next thing I knew, he'd been knocked back ten feet."

"Wait, what? Your power activated? You didn't tell me that! You should have led with that, hello! How was it? What did you do? Earthquake? Did you use plants to take him down? What?!"

"No," I said quietly, almost to myself. "It turns out, I don't have any earth powers."

"What do you mean? What did you do?"

"I'm a water fae, like my mom's grandfather, Yvain Le Fay."

"Oh, I remember him. He's really nice. So, water? Really?"

"Yeah. It's weird, right? I mean, we all thought-"

"Hold on, is that why Hollis named you Rain? Did he know?"

"No. Believe me, it was a total surprise to all of us. But I think I have had something to do with some of our more recent storms."

"No way. You can actually make it rain?"

"I think so. Maybe? I don't know. I'm going to have to get some lessons when I get to Aeden, that's for sure. The last few times I got really mad, lightning wasn't far behind. And I just meant to push Khai, not blast him with a ball of, of emotions, or whatever I did. So I guess the first thing I need to do is work on keeping my emotions in check."

"No offense or anything, but that's never been a problem for you before. You've always been so level-headed."

"Yeah. Well, now that my powers are acting up, I'm having a harder time with that. It's like... I can feel how other people are feeling sometimes, like an empath, you know? Honestly, if I didn't know better I'd think my hormones were out of whack or something, it's that easy to get knocked out of my happy place lately."

"Yeah, we kind of noticed, Rain," she teased me.

"Thanks, Legs."

"Anytime. If you need help staying stable, I'm here for you. Just call me your walking mood ring."

I laughed. "I'll do that, thanks."

"Good. So what's the deal with David, then? You want to tell me what really happened between you two, out there in the woods? How did you even end up out there, by yourself? Khai wouldn't explain."

I sighed. "No surprise there. It was kind of his fault."

"Really," she drawled. "Do tell."

I checked behind me to make sure David was still out of earshot. "Okay, so you know how I went to check out the old mill site by the barn my dad's friend Jonas told us about?"

Jules shook her head.

"Oh. Well, you and Khai were sleeping, I think, when I left. Anyway, I told Hollis where I was going, and I went for a swim."

"Oh, right. Khai asked us where you were when he woke up, woke me up, actually, and then he walked off to find you."

"Well, he found me. I was skinny dipping, and he went off on me, going on and on about how vulnerable I was, a powerless girl all alone in the woods, no elemental abilities, no clothes on, anyone could find me there, blah, blah, blah."

"He didn't."

"He did," I confirmed. "It really pissed me off. You should have seen his face, too, when I started to get out of the water. I thought he was going to have a heart attack."

"I bet."

"Anyways, I was so mad, I took off. I didn't mean to leave my GPS behind. I just wanted to be alone, cool off, you know? But I guess I was really mad, because that storm started up..."

"Holy crap. That was you? That was some intense weather, Ana."

"I know," I said ruefully. "Anyhow, that's how I found David. I was trying to find some place safe to wait out the storm, and I stumbled across this camp in the woods. There were yurts, like, the semi-permanent kind, and I saw a bunch of people going inside them to get out of the storm. They looked like normal people, I figured it was some sort of natural research outpost – I was pretty spooked by all that lightning, too. But when I ran into the closest building, I walked into a prison."

"No way."

"Seriously. There were like, I don't know, 8, 9 cells around the building? And they were filled with people. And David."

"Shut. Up. What did you do?"

"I let him out, what do you think I did? I let them all out. And then we ran."

"No way, Ana. What if David was some evil person or something? How could you know it was safe?"

"I guess I didn't, not really. But I trusted him when I met him before, and I trusted him then. Maybe it's a water fae thing? I don't know. Anyways, we all scattered, everyone took off in different directions, hoping it would make it harder for the warpers to track us after the storm. David and I, we were lucky Khai and Hollis found us."

"Do they know what happened?"

"No. At first they thought David attacked me, you should have seen how angry they were. But I made up a story, and they let him come with us. But I guess Khai never really believed me, after all, because he still doesn't trust David."

"Hmm. Well, I'm not sure that's all there is to it, with Khai, I mean. But that's a conversation for another day. You said something about warpers – who are these people? Why were they holding David captive?"

"Ah. Now that's the million-dollar question, isn't it?" I launched into an explanation about Starseeds, and aliens, and warpers. The whole time, Jules' eyes got wider and wider, and she kept looking back at David. Finally, I stopped to let him catch up and asked him to confirm everything I had just said.

"It's true, I swear," he said, backing me up.

"I don't know. This all sounds a bit far out to me," Jules said.

"Can you do something?" I asked David. "Show her your power?"

"I can try. I'm still learning how to use it, mostly I just astral travel when I'm sleeping, visit other people's dreams, that kind of thing, but let's see. I'll try something I've been working on."

He closed his eyes, and went very, very still. After a minute, Jules prodded him gently with one finger, and he swayed slightly on his feet.

"He's locked tight in place, like a tree. What is he doing?" she asked.

"This." David's voice came to us from behind, and I whipped my head around. "Hey, guys."

Amazed, I blinked rapidly, trying to process what I was seeing. "How did you? Wait-"

He was standing there, smiling at us, but he was also still standing where he had been, eyes closed.

"What the hell?" Jules jumped backwards, away from both Davids.

"Don't worry, I'm not going to hurt you. Some astral projectors can interact with the physical world when they travel, but I haven't figured that out yet. Even talking with you is a huge step forward for me – usually the waking can't hear me clearly."

"This is so freaky." Jules stepped forward and prodded David's body again, and then reached over and tried to touch his projection. Instead, her hand passed right through his arm. "Dude. What are you?"

"Um, that's we've been explaining for the last twenty minutes."

"I know, I know. But this. This is so weird. Wow. And I thought the fae had cool powers."

"Hey! We're cool."

"Yeah, yeah. Whatever," she waved me off, distracted by the novelty of passing her hand through David, again and again. His image started to flicker, and then disappeared. "Uh oh. Where'd he go? Did I break him?"

David laughed; a real, in your body, full belly kind of laugh.

"No, you didn't break me. I just can't hold it that long, not when I'm awake."

"Oh, too bad. Well, hey, you know, you should probably practice more," Jules shrugged.

"Jules is big on practice," I said.

"Well, yeah. How do you think I got to be a star soccer and lacrosse player? My great looks?"

"I kind of thought it might be your legs, Legs" David smirked.

"Not just my legs, wiseass. My running skills, and my stellar passing skills. Both of which I practiced, day in, and day out."

"She has a point," I sighed. "Maybe you can practice whenever we make camp? Assuming no one's around?"

"That's a great idea," Jules agreed. "You should practice, too, Ana."

"I don't know. My powers seem to come with some dangerous side effects.

"Your powers?" David asked. "I thought you didn't have any active powers."

"I didn't. Or I didn't know I did."

"And now you do?" he asked.

I nodded, and Jules filled in the blanks for me. "She's a water fae – that's what all that lightning and rain lately has been about. Her powers are tied to her emotions."

"And other people's," I added, grimacing. "And, I think, water."

"Huh. Well, if you want to try to practice, you can't hurt my astral form. At least, not if I keep it half-formed, like I just was."

"Wait, did you just offer yourself up as target practice?" Jules asked.

"I think I did," David grinned.

"I know Ana said you think you owe her, but dude, you're either braver or more stupid than I thought."

"How about we go with gallant."

"Oh jeez." Jules rolled her eyes. "I think I've had about all I can take. I'm taking point. See you aliens later."

Jules hiked off, leaving David and I laughing in her wake.

"She's right. We are both aliens." David said when he'd caught his breath.

"Well, if you get down to it, everything on this planet is alien. Heck, the planet didn't even exist before the fae got here and made it. Kind of calls everything into question, doesn't it?"

"Yeah. It redefines everything. Which is just another reason warpers aren't big fans of the fae. They don't like things they can't control to suit their own needs, or their own story. In this case, you guys kind of stole their thunder with that whole sunflare event."

"Hey, water fae here? I don't steal anyone's thunder." I held up my hands and wiggled my fingers. "I make it."

"Yes, you do." David looked at me, amused. "But seriously, warpers like to think they are better than humans. Better than the rest of us starseeds, too, since they've overcome 'the weakness of human morality.' Knowing that every person on the planet has alien ancestry on some level, and that the fae were here first, just as powerful as the original starseeds? That was a real blow for them."

"So?" I asked. We started walking as we talked, following Jules.

"So, they're planning something. They've *been* planning something."

"Like what?"

"I don't know. But the people in the other cells, they said they'd heard pieces, here and there. The warpers used to just want to control the governments, work behind the scenes and have all the power. Now, everybody gets along and everything is all kumbaya. There is no power to take. The only way to really have power, now, is to make it."

"You mean?"

"War," Ana. "They're planning a war."

Chapter 26

The next several days passed in a blur. The further north we got, the more arduous the climbs became, the more wild the trail. None of us had much breath for talking as we clambered up and down steep ravines, often using sapling trees as leverage. Thankfully, the rain stayed mostly at bay; any showers passing through were light and short.

Making camp fast became my favorite part of the day, and not because I was tired of hiking. Okay, well, maybe my muscles were screaming a little by the end of each day. But the more we'd hiked, the more sinewy I became. My body had adapted well to the rigors of the trail.

Each evening as the sun began to dip towards the horizon, I looked forward to the fun that I knew would ensue. Every night was the same. Make camp. Start dinner. Practice our powers.

Jules was both coach and referee, calling out the rules, giving us new ideas to try, judging if we'd done well enough to move on, or if we should try again. She didn't have any powers of her own, of course, but she had an inventive, calculating mind that made her perfectly suited to coaching.

"I think you've found your calling," I told her one night.

"Drill sergeant?"

"I was thinking more like teacher, but yeah, okay, that would work, too."

So far this evening we'd worked on David materializing enough so that he could touch me (he'd mastered a feather-light touch, which I thought was pretty exciting) and I'd been practicing guessing their emotions.

"Well, then, in that case – let's go again. David, it's your turn. Think of something or someone that evokes a strong emotion, you know what to do."

Jules stepped away, giving me some distance. We'd found that I picked up on strong emotions, but that proximity mattered, too. I didn't know if that was something that would change as my practice progressed or not.

David closed his eyes and his face relaxed. I closed my eyes, too, not wanting to pick up any clues from his expression. I calmed my mind, and allowed my own emotions to go blank. Slowly, the slightest tingle of warmth began to pass over me. It picked up in intensity, going from a bare tingle to a wave of heat. As it infused my being, I saw roses, pink and red, the petals wafting down all around me. I felt loved. No. I felt wanted.

Oh. My.

Very wanted.

I opened my lids, locking eyes with David. His gaze was heated, intense. Desiring. No one had ever looked at me like that before. Not Slice, not Tim. No one. This was the look of a man, not a boy.

I coughed, blushing. Jules was standing in the shadows behind David, watching me.

"Well?"

"I, um." What could I say? "It's something you like?"

"Something I really like," he confirmed in a low voice and I blushed.

"That's great," Jules clapped, coming forward into the light. "Good job, Ana. You're really getting good at this. Maybe we should try something new? See if you can pick out who's feeling what?"

I blinked, trying to dispel the feelings still radiating off David. His gaze didn't waver from mine, not until Jules sat down at his side and slapped a hand on his knee.

"Okay, think of something else. Ready, Ana?"

"Yes," I said, my voice coming out slightly strangled. Thankful for the low light, which hopefully hid my furiously rosy cheeks, I closed my eyes again. I couldn't center, couldn't focus. All I could feel was the remembered emotions David had been throwing at me moments before.

I took a deep breath and tried throwing up a block, a silvery ball of light to shield me, creating a clean slate all around me. At first, I felt lost. Adrift.

I allowed the isolation to settle over me, a feeling I realized I had never really felt, not for all my life. On some level, I must have been picking up empathically on people's feelings for years. I marveled at the realization, wondering what it could mean for me in the future.

But I was getting distracted. I needed to focus. I brushed my consciousness up against the ball of light, testing for weaknesses and finding none. No emotions. No connections whatsoever. I felt clear, cool, calm.

Gently, I imagined the silver shield thinning, and reached out with my mind towards Jules heart center. I felt joy, accomplishment. A rush of energy, like pride.

Interesting.

Still partially shielded, I was able to analyze the emotions without feeling them on such a personal level. Feeling detached, I turned my attention to David. Gently probing, again I felt warmth and a rush of energy. I cocked my head as if I was trying to hear better. I still couldn't get a read on the feeling itself, though.

David wasn't usually so hard to read. It was almost as if he was trying to hide his projections from me. Accepting the challenge, I thinned my shields a little more and imagined my heart center connecting with his on a thread of watery energy.

Instantly, I felt pulled from my own body, riding that thread like a wave, diving headfirst into his heart. There, I was tossed around, and my own heart constricted, as if gasping for space to breathe. I still couldn't see, but I could feel. I hardened my shields a bit, and felt my body right itself. Felt my body embraced. Warmed. No. Not warmed. Heated, as if by the sun itself. Energized, cocooned in a blanket of warmth and passion. Oh. I was the object of wanting, and I was completely and totally wanted. I started to feel warm hands on my hips, cool lips on my own.

"Okay, times up."

Jules' voice was like a bucket of cold water. Instantly, my shields fell, the line of water snapped, and I was back in my body, cold and alone.

I held my eyes closed, willing my heart to slow.

"Ana?" Jules asked. "You okay? Was it too much, trying both of us at once?"

"No!" I exclaimed, my eyes popping open. "It wasn't too much." I glanced at David, and realized what I was saying. "Well, maybe a little too much. It was a bit...intense, I guess?"

David made a face of mock woundedness, and I knew we'd be okay. I bit back a laugh, and looked at Jules. "So, um, I guess yours felt like... Victory?"

"Yes! I was remembering when I scored that goal two months ago, you know, the one right as the clock was running out against Deerfield?"

"Oh yeah! That was amazing. Wow. So I was right?"

Jules nodded enthusiastically. "What else did you get?"

I turned to David, whose eyes were dancing in the firelight as he looked straight into mine.

"Ah. Well, I guess it felt like you were really enjoying something?"

"Something I wanted for a long time, yes."

"Well, it couldn't have been that long," I retorted, thinking we'd only met a couple weeks ago. Chagrined, I slapped a hand over my mouth.

"What was it?" Jules asked, ignoring my outburst.

"Sorry, that's private," he said, winking at Jules.

"Aw, come on! You're not gonna tell us?"

"You heard him, Jules," I laughed. "It's private. Besides, it doesn't matter – I can't read thoughts. Just emotions, right?"

"How would I know? You're the fae here, not me," she said grumpily. Jules never had liked being denied anything. More than anything, she liked to win, and that meant getting her way more often than not.

"Aw, fine, don't be such a grump," David laughed, throwing an arm around my friend. "It was this dessert my grandmother used to make, before she passed."

"Really?" she asked.

"No."

"Oh!" She stood up and pushed him off his log at the same time. "You suck."

She was laughing though, and soon enough, we all were. If David and I shared a look while we all laughed, if I felt some of the heat and passion surround me again?

Well, who was I to tell?

Chapter 27

It was mid-day, and Jules was ranging far ahead of David and me.

We'd avoided talking about the night before, focusing on who we were, what we planned on doing over the coming months. Simple, innocuous topics. Except, of course, that every time I thought about the future, I wondered if I'd ever get to see him again. I knew where I was headed. Aeden, then McGill.

My future was set, at least for the next year or so.

David's, not so much. Beyond getting to safety in Montreal, he didn't know much about his future. Any ordinary life plans he'd had were shot now, or at least on hold. The warpers knew who he was, and they'd be looking for him. Most likely, he'd be set up with a new job and identity, probably working with the starseeds who fought to keep the warpers in check.

It was incredible to imagine that there had been this struggle between the two sides going on all these years. How could the fae not know about it?

It was a question I planned to pose when I got to Aeden.

I was thinking about just that when David grabbed my hand and pulled me to a stop.

"What?" I asked, surprised. "Did you hear something?"

I sent out my senses to scan the area, but all I picked up was Jules, far off and serene, and the local fauna, unperturbed.

"Can we talk?" David's brown eyes gazed down into mine, golden flecks of sunlight dancing within them.

"Isn't that what we were doing?" I asked, swallowing.

"Ana. I think you know what I mean."

"I- Yes. We can talk."

"Good." He exhaled with relief. "I hope I didn't upset you last night. You know, with the training we were doing."

"No, you didn't upset me. You just, sort of, surprised me. I wasn't expecting that. It took me off guard."

"It took me off guard, too. I was looking at the fire, just thinking about how warm and comfortable I was. You were there, on the other side, and I couldn't help watching you as you reached out. Did you know I can see auras, the astral energy around things?"

"No. I didn't know that. That must be so cool."

"It is. It was the first thing that started happening to me when my powers activated. Suddenly everyone was surrounded by these lights and colors. I'm still working out what it all means. Anyways, I never thought it could be useful at all, never thought it was important. Until you."

"Until me?"

"Yes. You have the brightest light I've ever seen, Ana. Maybe it's a fae thing, I don't know. But you glow like no one I've ever seen before. When you're mad, or happy, or sad. God. It's like watching the northern lights."

"Oh, come on," I laughed, blushing.

"No seriously. Ana, I knew you were special from the moment I saw you. But I didn't think I'd ever see you again. And then you showed up, and you saved me, and you've stuck by me all this way, and I don't know what I've done to deserve it but I do know that I want to. I want to deserve it. To deserve you."

"Me? But I'm not special. I'm just out of school, I haven't done anything in my life."

"Don't underestimate yourself, Ana. I think you're more than you know. And last night, you helped me again. You showed me something else about my powers that I didn't know I could do."

"What do you mean?"

"Last night, I started off thinking about my favorite cake, the one that my mom bakes on my birthday, and how good it would be to have some right then. I was thinking about it, and watching you get ready to read me. I could see your light radiating out and sifting through my energy, like cards being shuffled together. It's the only way I can describe it. And I didn't mean to do it, but in that moment all I could think was that I wanted more of that. More of you."

"David-"

"Wait, let me finish. I know I probably shouldn't be talking like this to you. Your brother would probably kill me. And Khai-"

"Khai is an ass."

"Maybe. I don't think so. I mean, we were lying to him. He was right. I think he just picked up on how I was feeling, and cares enough about you to want to protect you."

"Maybe," I said, chewing my lip. "But it's not his place."

"Then whose place is it?"

"Um, no one's? Mine? I'm not a child, you know."

"I do know," David's eyes darkened, and I felt rather than saw the shift in him. The heat was back, and the wanting. It was pouring off him in waves. "It's all I could think about last night. When I saw your shield go up it hurt. I thought, how will I ever reach her, if she can throw up a wall like that? And then you sent out that heart string towards me-"

"You could see that?"

"I could. And I think I might be able to learn to see other people do it, too. If I can do that, I'll be a real asset towards stopping the warpers. Maybe I could even identify warpers based on their auric fields before they turn. Who knows? But I'm getting off topic. I was supposed to be apologizing to you. I didn't mean to think of you like that, not while you were trying to read me. It wasn't right, and I'm sorry if I embarrassed you."

"You didn't embarrass me."

He cocked his head, and I laughed. "Okay, yeah, you did. But it's okay. Really." Whispering, I placed my hand over his heart. "It's okay."

I felt him coming near before he touched me, the heat practically irradiating me. And then, his lips were on mine, and we were kissing.

Had I thought kissing Slice was amazing?

What a fool I'd been. Now awoken as a water elemental, I could feel everything he was feeling as he kissed me, doubling down on my own tumult of emotions.

Overriding everything, was a soaring feeling of freedom, coupled with gratitude and gratification. I stopped myself trying to identify and separate every incoming strand of emotion, and just gave myself over to the ride.

The heavy weight of my pack was forgotten as I ran my hands up David's chest, delighting in the strength and muscle there as I went. Of their own volition, my palms found themselves cradling his cheeks, days-old stubble prickling my delicate skin.

He was delicious. Divine.

Beyond that, I couldn't form a coherent thought.

I'd heard my parents talk about telempathy, the sort of mental link between fae that shared the surge, channeling their emotions in great detail over the connection. I knew the surge went beyond what I was feeling, but I had to imagine it was close. Would all my kisses be like this, now that I'd awoken as a water fae? David was human, well, part anyways, and I wondered idly how that factored in. Was his starseed DNA an enhancement, in this case, or did it block my powers at all, the way their DNA had blocked The Flare from Anansanna? The thought only had a moment of my attention before I was sliding once more down the rabbit hole, reveling in the sensation of David's hands on my hips, his breath in my ear.

Had I really wondered if this could get any better? Any hotter, and I thought I might combust.

I was just thinking of how to remove my backpack without interrupting the flow of the kiss when I sensed another set of emotions approaching, like a sort of emo-radar I hadn't even really known I'd had.

The emotions were cold, like ice to my fire. Confident. Amused.

"Well, well, well. Why, David, you dog. And here I thought you were all search and rescue, and no play."

I stepped away from David, my pack throwing me slightly off balance as I spun to face the newcomer. Pitch black eyes with hair to match, a smile on his face that rose no higher than his lips.

"Cougan," David said, his eyes clearing. Without powers like mine to sense emotions, the man's arrival came as a complete surprise to David. He was still flushed from our kiss, his hair a mess. I imagined I looked about the same, but with crazier hair.

My hair was always crazier.

David's hands turned to fists and he stepped forward as if to shield me.

"What are you doing here?"

"Why, looking for you, of course. Well, you, and the rest of the rabble. It was pretty impressive, really, the escape you all made during the storm. Is this the girl that helped you?" Cougan's voice carried lilt to it, the song of the Irish, but he had none of the charm. "Tenzin told us how you all got out."

"You found him?"

"Him, and a few others. They have seen the error of their ways now."

"You mean they've been reprogrammed."

Cougan shrugged. "Potato, Potatoe. So, is this the girl?"

"It is," I said with a sneer, stepping up to David's side.

"Ana," he cautioned. "Stay back."

Cougan laughed. "Oh, that's rich. You think you're going to protect her? What, are you going to do, lure my soul into the astral world?" he derided.

"You can do that?" I asked David, surprised.

"No, he can't," Cougan sneered, reaching behind him and brandishing a gun towards us. "Which is why you are going to come with me. Both of you."

"You don't need the girl. She's just a human. Leave her alone, and I'll come with you."

"Oh, I think you both need to come with us. Ellen wants to have a talk with your little Ana, here. Plus, we could use some diversion at the camp, once we've finished setting up in our new location." He glared at me. "You've given us all a lot of extra work over the last week, lassie. I think you owe us a wee bit of fun, now, don't you?"

A frisson of fear snaked up my back, followed closely by a bolt of anger.

Just who did this guy think he was?

I had a feeling we were about to find out as he took a step towards us, gesturing with his gun.

"Now move."

"No," I said.

"Excuse me?" he wiggled a finger in his ear dramatically. I don't think I heard you correctly."

"I said, no. It's a complete sentence on its own. Do you want me to explain that to you?"

"This isn't a negotiation, girlie. Move, now. Or I shoot David here."

It only took one fraction of a second.

Cougan pointed the gun at David and I yelled, anticipating the shot.

"NO!" The word burst out of me with all the force of my anger and fear. Maybe I was still a little amped up from the kiss moments before, too. Who knew? But the strongest shockwave of emotion to come out of me yet burst out in all directions, ripping leaves off trees and knocking both men to the ground.

David was lucky. He landed in a patch of ferns by the trail that cushioned his fall. Cougan? Not so much. The burst of energy sent him tumbling backwards over a large stone, crash landing awkwardly against a tree. Instantly, a keening sound left his mouth, and the gun vanished from his hand.

"You broke my leg!"

"Serves you right, Cougan," David said. "Using your glamour powers to fake a gun? I can't believe I fell for that."

"Yeah." Cougan sneered. "You're pretty thick, mate."

"You mean, that wasn't even a real gun?" I asked, flabbergasted.

Cougan laughed at me and tried to get up, then fell back to moaning.

"You're clearly not human. What are you? A lifter?"

I looked at him, non-plussed.

"He means a starseed with telekinesis," David whispered in my ear.

I looked down at Cougan. "No. I'm fae. And thanks to you, your little warper secret is out of the bag. The Light Council will be hearing about this, soon enough," I said, referring to the governing body of the fae.

"Fae," Cougan spat.

"Yes. Well. I can't say this hasn't been fascinating, you know, meeting you and all, but I think it's time for us to move on. David?"

"Wait, what? You can't just leave me here. I'm wounded!"

"Tell me about it. Somehow, I imagine your friends have ways of finding you soon enough. Am I right?" I asked David.

"Definitely. Any traveler or mind reader worth their salt should be able to target a team member, within reason."

"Great." I turned on my heel and started to walk away, David following.

"But, you can't leave!" Cougan yelled after me. "You're fae. You don't leave people hurt in the woods! It's wrong."

I laughed. "Buddy, I don't think you get to lecture me on what's right and wrong."

Still, I did feel a twinge of guilt. I was a healer, and he was in pain. I could feel it, like a phantom ache in my own leg.

"Hold on," I muttered under my breath to David. I stalked back to Cougan and cocked my head, pondering him for a moment before squatting next to him.

I placed my hands on his leg, tempering the energy flowing through me to the right level.

"What are you doing?" Cougan squeaked, trying to back up further against the tree. Not caring about his peace of mind, I didn't bother answering.

Cougan whimpered, leaning his head back and closing his eyes.

"There. All done." I stood up, brushing off my hands. What I wouldn't have given for a shower right now. Touching him had made me feel dirty, like swimming through black oil.

"What did you do to me? Why can't I feel my leg?" he cried out as I walked back to David.

"Don't be such a baby. You can feel your leg, you idiot. You're just not in so much pain anymore. I wouldn't try walking on it though: I only eased your pain. The leg's still broken – in two places, if I'm correct." I flashed him a satisfied smile and linked arms with David.

"See you around, Cougan," I called out as we headed north on the trail.

"You can bet on it, Luv!" he shouted after us. "I'll get you both for this."

"You're welcome!" I yelled back, thinking maybe I should have left him in pain after all.

"Do you think that was wise?" David asked.

"I couldn't leave him in pain."

"I know, but healers are rare, even among pure-blood fae, aren't they?"

"So?"

"So, you're kind of a like a prize. At least that's how the warpers will see you."

I opted to process the compliment, rather than the warning.

"Why, thank you, David, that's so sweet of you to say. I don't think anyone's ever referred to me as a 'prize' before." I smiled up at him and batted my lashes playfully.

His gaze roamed over my eyes, my lips, and his pupils dilated. Then, he groaned.

"Ana. This is serious. If the warpers decide they want you..."

"They'll have the Light Guard to contend with, the most skilled warriors of the fae. And me. Don't underestimate me, David."

"How could I?" he asked, and laughed, squeezing my hand. "Still, let's catch up with Jules. The sooner we're out of these woods, the better."

Chapter 28

"Jules! Thank the gods, you're okay!"

I ran awkwardly, my pack bouncing from side to side, but I didn't care. I threw my arms around my friends, practically knocking her over.

"Whoa, easy there!" she chuckled. "Where's the fire?"

"Oh wow, you have no idea how worried I've been about you. Did you pass anyone else on the trail? Any guys?"

"No, no one. Why? What's going on?"

"The warpers, they found us. Well, one of them anyway. This guy came up on us while we were-" I broke off, blushing.

"You were...?" Jules asked with a gleam in her eye.

"Never mind." I wasn't ready to kiss and tell, especially not while David was standing right next to me. "We were on the trail and this guy, Cougan, he snuck up on us, tried to get us to go with him."

"The hot guy with the dark hair that was hiking with you before?" She asked David.

"I guess," David said, looking put out.

"Mmm. He was yummy," Jewels sighed. "So he's evil? Figures," she said, pouting.

"I guess. Anyways, he tricked us into thinking he had a gun, it was really scary. I'm glad he didn't come across you first."

"Speaking of that," said David, "I don't think we should split up again. We need to stick together, stay within shouting distance at least. Who knows who else is out here?"

"Ugh, that's a creepy thought." Jules shuddered. "How did you guys get away from Cougar?"

"Cougan," I said. "I blasted him with a big ball of 'No.' Not intentionally, but it worked. Knocked him on his butt. Poor guy broke his leg."

"Poor guy," Jules commiserated sarcastically.

"Yeah. I actually did feel a little bad. You know how I am. So I removed some of his pain, but left him with multiple breaks."

"You didn't!"

"I did."

"I am so proud of you." Jules high-fived me and I grinned.

"Yeah, well, his friends will find him soon enough, I'm sure. We really should get moving again."

"What about Hollis and Khai? Should we wait for them?"

I grimaced. "We probably should, I know that is what they would want, but I'm not ready to open that can of worms. Hollis is going to hit the roof when he finds out I knew about the warpers and I left anyway. Come on. And the warpers aren't looking for a couple of fae guys hiking through. They're looking for us. But we'll be okay. I can feel it."

"Really? Your water fae senses tell you that?"

"No. But I realized something today. I can feel people approaching, like a sort of emotional radar. Next time, they won't get the drop on us. If I sense anyone coming, we hide. Deal?"

"I guess. It's not like we've been seeing many people, anyway."

"Yeah. Hopefully it stays that way," David said and Jules patted his arm."

"Agreed," she said. "As hot as Mr. Wildcat was, I don't think I want to hang out with him, or his starseed friends."

"Definitely not," I agreed. "Except you, of course," I said to David, smiling.

"Hey, they're no pals of mine."

"I know," I sighed. "You know what I mean. Anyways, let's get moving."

Like robots coming off a charger, we all moved a bit awkwardly at first — I suppose we were each still in a bit of a daze, processing in our own way. Soon enough, we'd picked up speed, slowing down only when the trail demanded it. Steep barefaced rock ledges, narrow deer paths picking their way through boulder fields: the numerous hurdles of the northern end of Long Trail necessitated caution and dedication.

When we took breaks, we sat off the trail, out of sight. At night, we avoided staying at the shelters. If it was raining, Jules and I would share our tiny tent and David would sleep in his bivouac, a waterproof contraption designed to protect one person in a sleeping bag from the elements.

We ran across several solo-hikers and small groups, but the emotions I felt coming off them each time assured me they were safe. Weary, peaceful, happy — never cold, never the empty blackness I had felt coming off Cougan. Well, okay, one time there was this one young teen traveling with his dad, he had felt a bit grumpy and morose. But it was a benign, grudging kind of emotion, the sort you'd expect from most teens at his age. Plus, it had been raining when we'd come across them.

I knew how the kid felt.

At least this time, though, the rain wasn't linked to my own emotions. I seemed to have gotten that under control for the most part, and we continued our power practices each night with Jules. I enjoyed those evenings so much, the rare nights we sheltered with other people felt like a punishment from the clouds above.

So we stayed close to each other. We stayed safe. We moved quickly and made good time.

And, we stayed celibate. Any romance that had been popping up between David and me was dead in the water. Oh, there was a look from time to time, but with Jules always at our side we'd stopped flirting. It wasn't something we talked about, or even something I consciously decided to do. It's just, when you're looking over your shoulder all the time for the big bad, and you have a constant chaperone, romance kind of takes a back seat to real life, you know?

It wasn't long before we crossed the border between the states of Vermont and Quebec, the former United States-Canada boundary. The signpost marking the northern terminus began with a powerfully innocuous sentence:

A scenic trail that starts – ends here.

And they were right, the Green Mountain Club inscribers. Because this wasn't the end of anything. Not the end of what was going on with the warpers, and not the end of our hike.

At this point, in decades past most hikers would have turned onto the trail marked "Journey's End", which would take them out to a small parking area and North Troy Road, where they could reconnect with society. But since The Flare, the trail had gradually been extended on the Quebecois side, and now continued north past Montreal before turning towards Quebec and the open sea.

We had done it. I gazed across the north-western horizon where the sunlight sparkled upon the surface of the Missisquoi River and clouds danced dark shadows over the Sutton Mountains.

Oh, Canada.

Like a home-away-from-home, its energy had called to me since I was a young child. Partly, it was that we almost always traveled to Aeden via the remote woodland portal north of Montreal. But mostly, it was Montreal itself. I'd fallen in love with the French culture there. The rich food, so different from fae fare, which was light, fresh, and almost always vegetarian. The Victorian row houses and old stone buildings. And the smell. Somehow, it just smelled different in Montreal. My mom swore it was the proliferation of boxwoods used as hedgerows.

Me?

I thought it was the romance.

Dad said you can't smell romance, but I wasn't so sure. Thinking of it now, I wondered if maybe it hadn't been a portion of my water abilities manifesting early – the ability to smell the aura, the emotional imprint, of a place. Now, certainly, at the border post, I could feel the difference in the spot where I stood. So many people had passed through here, for so many different reasons. Some had burst into tears at the sight of Journey's End. Some had felt triumph. Some relief, and still more, regret, like they wished they could turn right around and do it again.

How did I know all this?

I was reading the land like emotional braille, the highs and lows radiating out from the rocks, the trees, even the signpost. Suddenly, I wondered if I shouldn't have given more credence to hauntings. Certainly, the emotions here had left their mark, easy to discern to anyone who had the tools within them.

It made me think more about the reality we lived in. So far, I had taken emotions at face value. But if they could linger in a place, without their original hosts? What did that mean about the fabric of reality? Were stones really just rocks, just dead matter, like some scientists said? Or were they alive, too, the way many fae and other cultures believed? Were their souls simply remembering, holding emotions, for those who wanted a record kept?

The more I used my water abilities, the more I learned about the starseeds, the less solid the world felt. Physical reality was tangible, but the energy that held it together was beginning to seem more real, more integral, to the equation than anything else.

Chapter 29

The wilds of the trail faded behind us, the rich forest smells, the vibrancy of the green leaves falling away in a dusty haze as we hitched a ride.

We'd come so far on the Northern Path, the Canadian extension of the Long Trail. But we couldn't go any further, not unless we wanted to walk to the ocean.

No, we'd had to leave the trail at last, following small access roads, dirt-worn and deep with ruts, until we'd come to a main thoroughfare. Although perhaps "main" isn't quite right. We'd walked for fifteen minutes along the pot-holed pavement before a motorcycle passed by, the loud growl of its engine preceding its arrival by a mile.

The noise was all show of course – oil burning vehicles were a thing of the past, and the majority of their noise had died along with them. For people who loved their vintage cars, conversion kits were available to upgrade to light energy. Only the slight susurration of the engines was allowed to remain, enough noise to alert pedestrians and prevent most accidents. Old habits die hard, though, and some people still installed noise-emulating machinery to their race cars and dirt bikes, small additions that could be disabled at will when the driver entered a noise-restricted zone.

Another ten minutes, and we'd hitched a ride in the back seat of an ancient surplus Humvee. Mostly obsolete, now that armies had been downgraded to civilian guards, the all-terrain military vehicle was no doubt quite useful in this rugged territory.

Francis, the owner of the Humvee, was more interested in the wildlife we had seen on the trail than how far or where we had hiked. An avid homesteader dedicated to living off the land, he spent most of his days hunting, leaving the rest of the farming and food production to his wife and three children. He was a pleasant sort, simple and honest. His emotional readout was bland, a relaxed state of ease and nothing else. Life was simple for Francis Leboutre, and he liked it that way.

He wasn't going all the way into Montreal; his business was at a tanning facility on the city outskirts, where he often brought his extra hides and remnants in exchange for a generous fee. The money from this trip would go towards a new wind turbine to power their pasture well, used to water crops and the family's small herd of dairy cattle.

Francis was a good provider, and he knew it, judging by the pride he took in his lifestyle, emanating off him like the halo of angels.

He dropped us off two blocks from the tannery, across the street from a monorail line that would take us right into the heart of the city. From there, we were just a short ride away from the old Light Guard safe house. It wasn't used anymore for official work, having been given over to my parent's friends, Ewan and Amber, as a wedding gift decades ago. They had offered it to us for the summer, a sort of home base to use as needed until Jules and I entered campus housing in the fall. My father had grumbled, wondering why we couldn't just stay with Hollis and Khai, who shared an apartment near campus, but my mother had laughed him off.

"Jules and Ana don't need any chaperones, stop being such a bear," she'd said at the time, kissing him on the cheek.

I was happy now that she had, even more than I'd been at the time. I know I had said we would talk to the guys when we got here, but I wasn't in any hurry to follow through on my plan. The longer it took to meet up with them, the better, in my opinion.

On the safe house's porch, I kneeled down and dug through my pack for the set of keys I'd stashed in one of the inner pockets.

"I can't believe Ewan and Amber are letting us stay here," Jules mused outside the Victorian building.

As a Light safe house, the home had been painted a mellow cream color for decades, its shutters once a respectable shade of dark green. Within, it had been decorated in minimalist shades of white, accents of green and blue sprinkled throughout. I'd seen the old pictures. Under Amber's artistic eye, the home had been transformed. The outside was now painted a vivid shade of periwinkle, the shutters dark plum, and the trim accents a rosy lilac. Every time I imagined Ewan lounging on the porch in his lumberjack shirts and rugged jeans, I had to laugh. Amber was such the perfect yin to his yang.

Successful at last, I held the keys aloft with a triumphant shout before unlocking the door.

Inside, the house continued to diverge from its former incarnation. The walls of the foyer had been painted a deep chocolate brown, a color that continued into the kitchen and eased gently into a warm plum in the living room. The furniture was made of rich synthetic leathers in varying shades of brown, pillows in peacock hues flung like jewels across their wide expanses. The furniture was a nod to Ewan's great stature – big, sturdy. An homage to masculinity. Amber would be dwarfed in the armchair, her body small and delicate as a youngling.

The three bedrooms were each decorated in vibrant shades, too: the Master bedroom a riot of greens and blues, another in reds and oranges, and the last in every shade of yellow you could imagine. It was in this room that I put my things, while Jules claimed the orange room. We gave David the main bedroom, since he would only be staying for one night and it was normally reserved for the masters of the house.

After that, we didn't reconvene for several hours. The lures of a real bathroom and a soft, private bed, was too much for any of us to ignore. I ran the water for a real bath and lay on top of my covers, waiting. Anticipating.

After my bath, I slipped into my last pair of clean underwear, wrapped one of the silken kimonos Amber left her guests around my body, and padded down the hall to start a load of laundry. After that, there was nothing for it. The bed was calling to me, luring me in with promises of bug-free, rainless sleep.

That was a promise I intended to see through, and I did.

It was well after sundown when I awoke. Still in the apricot-hued kimono, I walked back into the home's living area, where tall ceilings met over the kitchen and common areas, the two spaces divided only by a large butcher block island that also served as the dining area. Jules was sprawled on one of the couches in an oversized terry cloth robe, thumbing through an illustrated collector's edition of Bram Stoker's Dracula. I went to the fridge, hoping for a snack, but Jules shook her head before I could open it.

"Nuh-unh. Don't even bother. All that's in there is some jam and a packet of dried yeast."

I groaned and opted for a glass of water, instead.

"I did find these, though." She grinned holding up a bag of potato chips and a packet of chocolate cookies.

"Ooh, thank you, yes!" I happily rushed to join her on the couch, sitting where her legs had been a moment before.

"Any sign of David?" I asked, munching on one of the amazing cookies. When you are on the trail, such simple pleasures seemed a world away.

"Not a peep," she said, stuffing several chips in her mouth at once.

"Well, these cookies aren't going to hold me over long. I say we get dressed, go out and find something to eat. I'll wake David and let him know."

"Okay," Jules shrugged. "Hey, aren't our bags supposed to be here already?"

"Oh my gods, yeah, I totally forgot! But, where are they?" I wondered, hopping up and looking around. "They weren't in the hall, were they? I don't see them here, and they weren't in any of the rooms, right?"

"I don't think so," Jules said.

Inspiration hit and I threw open the double doors to the coat closet. There, half hidden amid jackets for every season and size, stood three suitcases, two very large and one small. A note was clipped to the handle of the carry-on, my name written in the looping scrawl of my mother.

I tore the envelope open and read:

Ana, my love,

I hope you have found your way to Montreal safely and had a fantastic time. I have managed to fit almost your entire wardrobe in these two bags – take the smaller one to Aeden, it has all the things you'll need there. You father and I will see you in a couple months, we don't want to miss your first day at school! Plus, I can see that we need to go clothes shopping, there's no way you'll make it through a Montreal winter with the coat you have now. Maybe you'll let me buy you another pair of boots, too? Amber will be around then, too, so I am sure she'll be able to steer us towards all the best shops. Though maybe I'd rather just keep you all to myself. Only a few days gone and I miss my baby girl so much already! Take care, give Airmed and all our friends kisses for us, and don't do anything I wouldn't do.

Love you,

Mom

Well, that was open-ended. But that was Mom. She had always said that if Hollis or I found ourselves doing something that we didn't think we could ever tell her, then we probably shouldn't be doing it. She was careful to explain that she didn't expect us to always tell her everything we did – she understood the way kids' minds worked – but if we didn't think we could tell her something, even if we had to? Then that was a good way to judge what we were doing. And you know what? I'd found she was right. I had no burning urge to tell her about what had happened between Slice and me, or that I'd tried some Roumkivara 'shine, but I knew I could talk to her about it if I ever needed.

I wondered about the sort of things I wouldn't be able to tell her about, and found myself shuddering. Becoming a warper, killing someone on purpose, destroying someone's happiness forever: those were the sorts of things I imagined wanting to hide. Actions that were unfathomably evil to me, things no one should ever have to admit to.

I shook the dark thoughts from my head, following Jules as we dragged the suitcases toward our rooms. Remembering that I had meant to wake David, I walked back to his door and raised a hand, about to knock. Loud, trembling snores rumbled their way through the wood, and I bit back a smile. Not having the heart to wake him, I lowered my hand. I could get him after I'd dressed.

Pretty soon, the poor guy would be facing a lot of questions. Whatever issues my family might have when I finally came clean about the starseeds, his own people were sure to be far more worried about what was going on. After all, it was their war, not ours.

Or at least, it had been. If a league of evil warpers was bent on disrupting the peace that Anansanna and my mother had wrought, surely the Light Council would have something to say about it.

I frowned, contemplating the clothes in my bag along with my future.

Things were going to change, and I wasn't sure how I felt about any of it.

Chapter 29

I wound a curl of reddish hair around my finger and released it, testing its bounce. The month of hiking had lightened my locks to a more vibrant rust tone, less brown than it had been, more the color of my youth.

As a baby, my hair had been so fair and fiery, my father had said he was worried I would combust if he set me too close to the wood stove. As I'd gotten older, though, the color had darkened, faded, with every year. Like life was dulling my spark.

Had the long walk had brought it back? Most likely it was all my time in the sun, so much more than I was used to. Though maybe, just maybe, my spark had been reignited. Perhaps the danger had done it, or the acquisition of my powers. Or maybe, it was the attentions of a good man, as brief as they had been.

There I was, being fanciful again. I stuck my tongue out at my reflection, and the minx in the mirror did the same to me. Her eyes were bright, like spring grass in the rain, and a spray of fresh summer freckles spread across her nose and cheeks, visible against the lightly tanned skin. Her eyes were lightly rimmed in grey kohl, giving her a slightly mysterious, playful air.

Of course, she was me. I'd put on a simple white camisole, decadently fresh and clean from the bag my mother had packed, along with yellow espadrilles and a short, gathered skirt covered with blue and yellow daisies. Knowing the summer evenings could be cool in the north, I had a light blue cardigan already laid out on the bed, ready to slip on when we left.

First, I needed to wake up David. I padded down the carpeted hall to his room and listened. The snores had quietened, less rumbly, now more like a kitten's purr.

Rather than knock, I opened the door. The drapes were closed, casting the room in near blackness, David's form just barely discernible against the pale sheets. I crept over and stared down at him, allowing my eyes to adjust to the light. It hit me that now, as a water fae, I would never be able to see in the dark, the way my parents both could. That power was for earth fae only. But I could sense emotions, and David's were content.

He looked so peaceful, so relaxed. I just didn't have the heart to wake him. We could grab him something to eat while we were out. I couldn't imagine the strain he'd been under, the fear when he'd been captured, the shock of finding out your own relative had crossed over to the dark side. Being on the run.

No. He needed to rest. I turned to go, took a step away, but was pulled back. Pulled down.

A muffled squeak escaped my lips as I found myself suddenly, inexplicably, lying across David's warm, bare chest. Staring into his cool, clear eyes.

"Hello," he said.

Less of a word, more of a thrum that traveled all the way through me.

"I didn't want to wake you." I meant to speak plainly, but it came out as more of a whisper.

"Mmm," he murmured against my ear. "Too late."

And then we were kissing, and the feelings rolling through me were intense, on fire. It felt amazing to be wanted, wholly appreciated, in this way. For gods knew how long, I reveled in the feeling, giving myself over to it entirely. Letting go of all thought, and just allowing myself to feel what he was giving me.

I'd never known how good it could be to feel desired in this way, and it washed through me like a drug, the euphoria, the high.

My body, however, had some needs of its own, my stomach gurgling loudly, bringing me back to myself. I raised my lips off David's just a hairbreadth away, pausing, blushing. It growled again, and David's answered, chorusing like two wolves fighting over a bone, and he chuckled.

"I suppose we better do something about that," he mused.

"That's actually why I came in here, to wake you up for dinner. Jules and I were planning to head out soon."

I eased off him, smoothing down my skirt as I stood. He placed a hand casually on the back of my knee, running a hand along my thigh.

"Any chance we could order in?" he asked, raising an eyebrow with a gleam in his eye.

"I don't think so," I said ruefully. "Jules is pretty set on having a night out."

"Right. Okay, well, I'll try to find something clean in my pack."

"Ah, sorry. We should have grabbed your clothes to wash before you crashed. But maybe you can fit into something of Ewan's, I'm sure he wouldn't mind." I gestured to the closet. "Help yourself."

"Are you sure?"

"Totally. Though I must warn you, he's kind of a giant."

"Okay, I'll see what I can do." He sat up, swinging his legs over the bed, and paused. "You should probably go now." He gestured to the sheet draped across his legs, and I realized he wasn't wearing anything underneath.

"Oh!" I backed up, and hit the door. "Right. Yes. Okay – I'll just, um, wait out here. In the living room, I mean, not outside your door." My eyes widened and I realized how ridiculous I sounded. Rolling my eyes at my own idiocy, I turned and rushed from the room. When I plopped down on the couch, Jules peered at me and instantly broke out laughing.

"What?"

"You look like a crazy person, between that look on your face and your hair..." she broke off, still laughing.

I ran a hand over my hair, smoothing it down. "Shut up."

"So, David's awake, I take it?" she teased me.

"Yes, he's going to try and find something clean to wear in Ewan's closet."

At that, she burst out laughing again. After a moment, I joined in.

"I know, it's ridiculous, right?"

"Oh my God, I mean, David's no slouch, but Ewan's just huge."

"I know!" I heard a door click and shushed her. "He's coming."

Sure enough, here he came, wearing some halfway decent khaki climbing pants and a plain black tee. The shirt was fitted, showing off muscles that moved in his arms as he walked, muscles I had been tracing with my palms just moments before. He looked good.

"You found that in Ewan's room?" Jules asked.

David ran a hand over the shirt. "The pants are mine. You weren't kidding about how big the clothes would be. But I found this tee in the back of the closet, with this jacket."

He held up a black motorcycle jacket, and I realized he was wearing a shirt of my dad's. My parents came up here often enough on weekends, it should have occurred to me they might have left some clothes here.

"Hey, isn't that-?" Jules started and I cut her off.

"Yes, it is." Suddenly, I wasn't feeling quite so turned on by the shirt's tight fit. I smiled awkwardly and stood up. "Well, if we're all ready? I'm starving."

Jules popped up, always ready to go, and we headed outside, into the cool night air.

Chapter 30

The evening passed in a blur of bright lights and laughter. Being off the trail, cloaked in the anonymity of the city, it felt like all our cares were gone.

They weren't, of course. But it was good to let go, to just enjoy the bounty Montreal had to offer. David had never been to the city before, so Jules and I made sure he had the best introduction. First, we hit a small neighborhood café that had opened several years before, ordering savory Breton-style crepes with salmon and crème fraiche inside the incredibly thin, yet hearty, buckwheat pancakes. We washed them down with bottles of Quebecois hard cider, a traditional pairing. When David started looking at the menu again, ready to order a second round of crepes, Jules stopped him.

"Not here. We have to go to Gerard's."

"Who's Gerard?"

"Not who," I said. "What. Gerard's has the best poutine in old town."

"Poutine? That's not, like, some kind of liver pâté, is it? Because I don't do liver."

I laughed. "No. Poutine is completely inoffensive, unless you have a cholesterol problem. How's your HDL?"

"After weeks on the Long Trail? I think I'm good," he said with a grin. "What is it?"

"You'll see." I winked.

An hour later David was leaning back in his chair at Gerard's, moaning as he rubbed his slightly rounded stomach.

"That. Was. Amazing."

"Right?" Jules agreed, polishing off her beer. We had just finished a four-person platter of "Poutine Gerardoise": large French-style fries laden with rich beef gravy, fresh cheddar cheese curds, and farm-raised lardons, thickly sliced bits of salt pork. Everything was farm-to-table, harvested from Gerard Malbec's own land outside the city. Poutine may have begun as a cheap way to keep fat on the bones during hard Northern winters, but it had become a hallmark of Montreal nightlife, something sustaining for the dance-all-night youth of the city.

We paid our bill, unable to even glance at the dessert menu, and left.

The rest of the night, we club-hopped. We started slow with Irish ballads at Clancy's, and ended hard with tribal beats at Zora's.

Z's was practically an institution at this point, a fae stronghold of dancing and fun since before my mom's time. Close to the house, it was the perfect place to end the night. Plus, it always had the best music; local spin-masters who knew how to keep a crowd dancing. The fact that all the employees were fae was just a bonus.

I hadn't realized that I'd missed being around other fae this past week, not until they were everywhere. Their emotions rang through louder, more clearly than that of any human's. At first, it took me by surprise. I adjusted my empathic shields, so I wouldn't be overwhelmed by the lightness I was feeling. Still, I felt slightly giddy, almost as if I had been drinking 'shine and I couldn't help giggling as I dragged my friends out onto the dance floor.

Feeling less inhibited than normal, I allowed myself to be swallowed by the crowd. Normally, I would have made sure I knew where my friends were, that I stayed close to them, like a duckling hides under the wing of her mother. But tonight, I didn't care. This was my safe place. These were my people. Oh, sure, there were humans here, too. With a slight shock, I realized some might even be starseeds, and opened my eyes. I reached out with my senses, searching for any sign of danger. I touched my holo-chat nervously. I should have called my dad, let him know we'd arrived. I knew he was keeping tabs on our location remotely, but still – it would have been the smart thing to do. The daughter-ly thing. A month ago, I wouldn't have needed to be reminded, he would have been foremost in my mind. Not an afterthought. I felt a moment of empathy for my parents, understanding for the first time what my growing up really meant for them.

Then, I shrugged. Now wasn't the time to mourn my childhood. At least I'd remembered to bring the chat. I could call him in an instant if I needed to.

My emotions reeled as the crowd's own feelings steamrolled over me. I tensed, bracing for any signs of coldness, the hardness I had felt from Cougan, but I felt none. The club was warper free. Sighing with relief, I smiled, and picked up the beat of the music again. A young fae, close to my age, caught my eye and grinned.

Taking my smile as an invitation, he made his way over, matching his moves to mine without touching.

"Water fae?" he leaned in and asked, like he already knew the answer.

"Yeah. How did you-"

"Me, too. I felt you the minute you walked in."

I raised my eyebrows and he put up his hands. "Not a line, just an observation."

"Can you tell everyone's element?"

"Not everyone. But the way you puffed up with all the input in here, and then dropped your shields, that's kind of a dead giveaway."

"Oh. I just found out I was water fae a couple weeks ago, I'm still figuring all this stuff out."

"That's cool. You live in the city? We should hang out. I've had mine for three years now; I could help you."

I eyed him, assessing. He seemed genuine, and his smile was infectious. He had the fine look about him that humans seemed to associate with all fae, like Legolas in the old Lord of the Rings movies from my parents' youth.

"Is that a line?"

"Will you say no if it is?"

I looked around, thinking of David. I wasn't sure what it was we had, but I wasn't normally the flirtatious type.

"I don't know," I said honestly.

"Truth, that's good. Look, my name's Gawen. I'm a student at McGill, I share a flat nearby with some friends. Give me a call sometime, if you want to hang out, maybe practice your powers." He pressed a button on his holo-chat, and I heard mine ping in response, storing his number.

"Thanks. I'm actually starting at McGill this fall. I'm supposed to go to Aeden for a while for some training first, though."

"Oh, that's cool. Maybe you'll be able to teach me some things then, when you get back."

He flashed me a charming grin, and I laughed.

"You have a great laugh," he said, leaning in to whisper against my ear. The music had slowed, and people were leaving the floor. His hand came around my waist. "And yes, that was a line. Can I have this dance?"

"I-"

I didn't get a chance to consider the dance, because just then a cough startled us both, and David was at my side, frowning.

"Mind if I cut in?"

"Not at all." Gawen stepped back without looking away from me. "I never caught your name."

"Ana."

"Ana," he repeated with that elven gleam in his eye. "I'll see you around, Ana."

He winked at me, and was gone.

"What was that about?"

David grumbled, pulling me to him, engulfing me in his space. I could feel his displeasure, and it stung me, almost as much as it gave me a rush, knowing he'd been upset to see another man flirting with me.

"He's a water fae, like me," I said, feeling slightly uneasy. It wasn't really my place to discuss another fae's powers. Generally considered a private matter among fae, it was, at the least, slightly bad manners for me to do so. David deserved an explanation, though. "He sensed what I was when we came in."

"Oh. So it's a fae thing? Like welcoming you to the area?"

That wasn't quite it, but it gave me an easy way to change the subject. "Yeah. Pretty much. I scanned the crowd, you know, for warpers. We're safe here."

"Good to know. Though I'm not so sure that's entirely true." He pulled me closer, looking down into my eyes. "I'm pretty sure your welcoming committee thought you were tasty looking. And he's not the only one."

He winked at me, a predatory gleam in his eye, and I laughed. "You're so full of it. Just dance, you geek."

I placed my arms around his neck and leaned my head against his chest, relaxing as we swayed. A familiar scent washed over me, the fabric spray my mom always used still stored in the fiber of my father's forgotten shirt, and I inhaled deeply.

"You smell like home," I said without thinking.

I opened my mouth to explain, but shut it when I heard his reply, the barest whisper against the top of my head.

"So do you."

Anything I would have said then, died on my lips. Instead, I held him tighter, and closed my eyes.

Sinking into the known, and the unknown.

Chapter 31

Heavy footsteps and a bang brought me to my senses.

I opened my eyes, blinking heavily, and looked up to see the outline of a man in the doorway.

"Out. Now." Words ground out in frustration, anger, brooking no argument.

A second silhouette appeared, along with a string of curses.

"You have got be fucking kidding me."

I started to sit up, to wipe the sleep from my eyes, but a warm arm came around me and held me back. David sat up, shielding me with his body.

"Ever hear of knocking?" he said mildly.

We'd fallen asleep together the night before, tumbling into bed amid laughter and exhaustion. Before I could even think about how far I wanted it to go, we'd both passed out, tangled together like octopuses spooning.

Khai and Hollis advanced towards the bed, and I swear one of them was growling. Sparks flared off Khai's fingertips, bright in the shuttered room.

"Crap, is he okay?" David whispered to me, loudly enough for everyone to hear.

Hollis looked at Khai and hissed. "Dude, rein it in."

I rolled my eyes and sighed. "Stop being so dramatic, both of you. Nothing happened, not that it's any of your business."

They paused, halfway across the floor.

"Seriously?" Hollis asked.

"Seriously. Now, get out of my room," I ground out. "Now!"

Looking sheepish, Hollis turned and left. Khai followed, only to stop at the door. Without looking back at us, he said, "You have two minutes."

And then he left.

Without closing the door.

"What a jerk," I muttered.

David chuckled. "Well, that's one way to wake up. More effective than an alarm clock, for sure."

"You're taking this very well," I grumbled. I'd take an alarm clock any day. Heck, I'd take a fire drill over what had just happened.

He wrapped his arms around me and kissed my neck. "I woke up with you in my arms, didn't I?"

"Mmm. Good point." I smiled and kissed him back. "Well, I guess we'd better face the day."

Reluctantly, I rolled out of bed, smoothing down my skirt and hair. Despite falling asleep in my clothes, a quick check in the mirror showed I wasn't too much worse for wear, minus some dark smudges under my eyes which I was able to wipe away with a tissue. David pulled on his t-shirt and took my hand.

"Come on, I smell coffee."

We walked into the hall, practically bumping into a tired looking Jules, wrapped in a delicious looking kimono that set off the golden tones in her brown skin. Hollis, I thought, eat your heart out.

"They make you get up, too?" She yawned.

"Yep," I answered.

"Jerks."

"Yep."

Massive cups of coffee sat on the counter, steaming with their lids off. An open box next to them held beignets, Montreal's refined answer to the American doughnut. I reached for one gooey, sugar-crusted confection and bit in, sighing.

"At least you brought food," I sighed, glaring at Hollis.

"Here," Khai said, without looking at me. "We got you a hot chocolate, too."

"Oh, thanks," I said, unable to hide the pleasure from my voice. Coffee had never really done anything for me, but chocolate...

"Yes, this is great, thanks, guys," David said agreeably, taking a long sip of his coffee.

"Yeah, well, we didn't do it for you," Khai snapped, and walked away from the island to sit on a couch by himself.

Hollis sighed. "Okay, why doesn't everybody grab what they want, and take a seat. I think we need to clear the air."

Jules snorted, but did as he'd asked. I smirked at him, mouthing "You're doomed," as I passed. It was a false threat, however. I knew that what I'd hid from them was worse than anything he'd done to Jules. Nerves lit my stomach, and I tried to quell the tension I felt with another beignet as I sat next to Jules on the couch across from Khai. David perched on the arm next to me, and Hollis sat in the chair between the couches. Did he see himself as a mediator, I wondered? Mr. Perfect, always in charge.

No one spoke at first, and I used the moment to feel out the emotions in the room. There was a lot of anger there. Mistrust. Hurt. Envy.

Envy?

Where was that coming from?

Before I had a chance to fine tune my empathic sensing, Hollis spoke up.

"Look, I know you guys are mad at us, and we've talked about what happened and we agree that we didn't handle things well back at camp." He looked at Khai for confirmation, but Khai was stone-faced, looking at a point above my head on the wall.

Jules crossed her arms and sighed.

"Go on."

"I think everyone can agree that things were said they didn't mean. We're all friends here-"

"Not all of us," Khai said quietly, still looking at the wall.

"We're all friends here," Hollis repeated, "and we all care about each other. Being on the trail, maybe it just made everything more intense. I think we were all worn a bit raw, you know. The important thing, is that we can move past this, and stay friends."

He looked around the room, trying to place peacemaker, but no one spoke.

Finally, Jules sighed, a deep, weary sound. Suddenly, a new feeling had been added to the mix. A heart breaking.

"Oh, Jules," I whispered. I reached out to hold her hand as she spoke.

"Right. Friends," she said over-brightly. "Of course. Well, I think it's only fair that we share some of our side of the story with you. You're right that tensions were high on the trail – but you don't know the whole story. Ana? David? You want to tell them, or should I?"

"Tell us what?" Hollis asked, perplexed. The shift in Jules had thrown him, I could tell. I wanted to smack him for being such an idiot, for breaking my friend's heart all over again. But now wasn't the time. David and I needed to come clean.

"I'll do it," I said. Khai was looking me in the eye now, sitting forward in his seat, and I couldn't look away.

"You sure? I can-"

I cut David off. "I've got this."

I exhaled, taking a moment to decide where to start. Like a whisper, I heard my father's voice in my head. Words he'd whispered so many times while we worked out problems side by side.

Go back to the beginning, Ana. If you can't see your way, always go back and retrace your steps. You'll find the answer on your way.

"I guess I'd better start at the beginning. That day when you found me at the waterfall, remember, and we had that fight?"

Khai nodded, his jaw tight. "I remember."

"Well, when I ran off, I was so mad. My powers called in that storm, only I didn't know what was happening, and I was so scared. I just kept running, looking for a place to wait it out. That's when I stumbled upon the camp."

"Camp?" Hollis asked. "What camp?"

"The camp where I found David." I smiled, trying to ease what was coming, and David took my hand.

Khai's eyes narrowed, suspicious. "I thought you said you found David on the trail, with a broken ankle or something. Isn't that what she said, Holl?"

"Yeah," Hollis said slowly. "It is."

I swallowed. "I'm sorry. I couldn't tell you. I didn't want to ruin the trip and I knew... Well, let me tell you the rest of the story, okay."

"Fine. We're listening." Hollis sat back, arms folded across his chest like an emperor waiting to pass judgment.

"The camp was huge. Several yurts and a whole bunch of tents. People were freaked out by the storm, and everyone was heading into the yurts. I figured it was some sort of nature research facility, you know, a field camp like the ones we've been to with Mom and Dad. I ran into the closest building and found all these cages, but there weren't animals inside them at all."

"What do you mean?"

"There were people in the cages, Holl. It was some kind of jail, and you could tell the prisoners weren't being treated well, either. I would probably have run out of there right then, storm or no storm, except I saw David, and I knew I had to get him out of there, along with everybody else."

"Jesus, Ana," Khai said. "What if you-"

"I know. It was crazy stupid, I'm sure. But I was able to open all the cells and then we all scattered, hoping by the time the warpers found us gone they wouldn't be able to track us in the rain."

"Warpers?"

"Right, I haven't gotten there yet. So, anyway, David really did have a messed up ankle, so I healed that first and then for a while we just ran as fast as we could in the direction I'd come from. I knew with your earth powers you'd find me eventually, once you got worried enough to look. Eventually, we slowed down and that's when David explained what had happened to him."

"Which was? Because, you know I love you, but this all sounds a bit crazy. I mean, things like this just don't happen anymore, not since The Flare," Hollis said.

"It does. It always has," David said. "Just, no one really knows about it."

"What's he talking about, Ana?" Khai asked.

"I'm getting there. But first, I guess I need to ask you both: how much of the old stories do you really believe? About the Ancients, and how we got here?"

Hollis made a face. "How we got here? You mean that whole Ancient spaceship story? I guess we kind of have to believe it, since Mom saw it when she bonded with the Tree of Life. But it's always sounded like a crazy alien fairy tale to me. Why? What gives, Ana?"

"Well, it turns out we're not the only aliens on the planet."

"Huh?"

"Hollis, Khai, I'd like to introduce you to David Montauk, Starseed. Friendly Alien. Astral Traveler." I proudly waved a hand towards David and grinned. David blushed and rolled his eyes, while Khai and Hollis just gawked at us both.

Khai was the first to recover.

"I'm sorry, you're saying aliens really exist, and he's one of them? And he was being held captive by, who, the government? Like E.T.?" The disbelief in his voice cut through me, mocking me, but I could sense the hurt and fear on the other side of it. Only that allowed me to remain patient.

"No. By other starseeds. Turns out the aliens came here several thousand years ago. They came for a visit, and like a lot of tourists who overstay their welcome, they had children with the locals. The Nommo, that's what they were called then, they had all kinds of psychic powers, and a lot of people thought they were like Gods."

"Seriously? Where were we? How come the fae don't know about this?" Hollis demanded.

"Are you sure they don't?" asked David.

"Maybe the Light Council does know. I don't see how they couldn't. But the Nommo are gone. All those powers they had were being passed on to their kids, their starseeds. Some of the starseeds used their powers badly, like Dark fae, and humans didn't like it. Wars were fought, and the Nommo left the planet, hoping that would be enough to undo the damage they'd done. I wouldn't be surprised if the Light even had something to do with talking them into leaving. Anyway, those bad seeds? The Nommo couldn't take their children with them, and the starseeds went into hiding. They started policing their own people, trying to teach young starseeds how to use their powers wisely. Sometimes the power would go to their heads, warping their morals and their minds, and they'd get greedy. When that happens, they're called warpers, and they're still around."

"Okay, I can sense there is a bigger story there around these warped people, but there's something I don't get." Hollis stood up, pacing. "How can they still be a problem? I mean, when The Flare happened, all the Dark fae become Light again. Humanity shifted towards a more peaceful society. Why not these seeds?"

"Starseeds," David corrected.

"Whatever."

"We don't know," David answered, sounding annoyed. "As best we can figure, Nommo DNA seems to cancel out most human DNA, even when a person is half human. And since your red sun was made to work with fae DNA, and all life on earth comes from Anansanna and the Tree of Life..."

"The Flare didn't work on you," Khai finished.

"Afraid not," David shrugged, looking less than apologetic. "Especially not on the warpers."

"So, tell us about these warper guys. What do they want?" Hollis asked, suddenly all business.

"Power. Money. Control. Everything the Dark wanted, from what Ana's told me," David said.

"You know, she's named after Anansanna," Khai said, pointing at me, suddenly off-topic.

"So?" I asked.

"So?" he retorted, and glared at David. "She's special. Like her mom. You really think you should be dragging her into whatever issues your people are having with each other?"

"Khai!" I exclaimed, shocked. "Will you ever stop treating me like a little kid? David hasn't dragged me into anything. I want to help him. As should you."

"Unfortunately," David interrupted, "I don't think the warpers are just interested in starseeds, either. Since The Flare, they've had to adapt to a whole new world, just like everybody else. The only thing is, they don't like this utopia you've brought about. Up until now, they've always been reluctant to go against the fae, there are so many more of you and your powers are so much bigger than ours in so many ways, but now..."

"Now what?" Hollis asked.

"Something's changed. From what I heard at that camp, they're building an army. Capturing and mind-warping more innocent starseeds every day. That's what they were doing in the woods. Who knows how many of them there are now. But I can tell you, my cousin isn't the only one who's disappeared without a trace, only to become a warper."

Just thinking about it, a mind being turned like that, gave me the chills.

Khai saw me shiver, and he asked if I was okay, just as David put an arm around me, rubbing my shoulder.

"I'm okay. Just, I've seen what these guys can do. I've talked to them. The thought of someone like that being in control of the whole world, or even a city..." I shook my head. "It's too much."

"Wait, what do you mean you've met one?" Hollis walked over and knelt in front of me, his eyes roaming over me as if he was examining me for marks. He wouldn't find any. "I thought you guys outran them in the woods?"

"We did. But later, on the trail, we ran into Cougan, one of the guys David had been hiking with."

I looked at him, and he took up the story.

"Yeah, turns out my cousin's boyfriend was a warper, and so were his friends. The hike they took was all part of a plan to get her on their side. Then, since I wouldn't stop looking for her, they'd decided they'd turn me, too. Thank God your sister showed up when she did. She saved my life."

"And you? What did you do? No please, don't answer that. All you've done is put her in danger," Khai said with a sneer. He looked me in the face, again. "Did he hurt you?"

"David? No! Of course not."

"Not David, Cougan," he said in a softer voice, but the angry edge of concern was still there.

"No," I said, flustered. "Actually, I hurt him. I didn't mean to, but I blasted him with an empath wave when he threatened us with a gun, and he fell and hurt his leg. We left him for his friends to find. He was pretty pissed, but I'm sure he'll live."

Khai stood and looked at Hollis, whose face had turned hard. An unspoken communication passed between them and Hollis walked over to his pack.

"What are you doing?" I asked, a bad feeling coming over me.

"What I should have done a week ago," he said, holding up his holo-chat. "No. Scratch that. What you should have done. I can't believe I let you walk off into the woods by yourselves. This thing, whatever's going on? It's too big for us. I'm calling Mom and Dad."

Chapter 32

It was the longest morning of my life. After a brief talk with Hollis, both my parents made me explain what had happened via conference call. About halfway through my second retelling, things started getting noisy, while my parents got quieter.

"Um, what's going on?" I asked. "What's all that noise in the background?"

"What do you think, Ana?" my father said in a quiet voice. The voice he used when he was disappointed in me. I hadn't heard it often growing up, but when I did it never boded well for me. "We're packing."

"You have ten hours, Ana," my mother said helpfully, her voice muffled and distant. Probably deep in the hotel closet. "I suggest you take your friend to that headquarters you mentioned before we get there. Your father is looking rather daunting at the moment."

I cleared my throat nervously. "Right. Sure, of course. I'll go right now."

"No, young lady, you will not. You will finish the story you were telling us. I believe you said you'd been practicing your new powers with Jules and David?"

"Yes." I sighed, and launched into a step by step account of our time on the trail after we separated from Khai and Hollis. My father was livid, I could tell, but at least he wasn't interrupting me. Much. The whole time, Khai paced back and forth next to the couch I was on, while David held my hand supportively. Jules had disappeared to her room, and Hollis had signed off, going out to the porch for some air. When I got to the part with Cougan, Khai groaned.

"Will you stop that?" I exclaimed, turning on him.

"Stop what?"

"Making all that noise. I can't think with all the pacing you're doing, you're driving me nuts."

"Good. You're driving me nuts, too." He glared at me, but at least he sat down, positioning his body away from me as he rested on the arm of my sofa. I couldn't see his leg bouncing up and down, but I could feel it.

"Ana? I'm waiting." My father's voice grated over the line, and I set my mind to ignoring Khai. The small pulses of anxiety coming from him weren't making it easy, but I threw up my shields and plowed on with my tale, finishing it a second time.

And then a third.

My father was nothing, if not thorough.

Finally, just as they were getting on a specially chartered plane to head back stateside, my parents signed off, and I stood up to stretch.

"We'd better go." I groaned as I leaned into another stretch, trying to release all the tension I was feeling from David and Khai, never mind my own.

"Alright. I'll pack my stuff."

David headed off toward the laundry and I turned to Khai.

"And you. Dude, can you chill out, please? Your anxiety is giving me heartburn, I swear. And all that bouncing you're doing is making me motion sick. At least go and sit over there." I waved at the other couch.

"Maybe if you'd spent more time practicing your shielding, and less time making out with your new boyfriend."

"Watch it, Khai. You're on dangerous ground."

"Am I?" He settled down across me, and watched me through hooded lashes.

I glared back at him.

"Fine," he said after a minute, looking away. His voice had gone cold, indifferent. "Just get rid of him, like your mom said. It's not safe for him or us to have him around."

"Whatever. I'm going to get dressed."

"What, don't want to parade your walk of shame clothes in front of Alec and Siri?" he mocked.

"Shut up. I'm not ashamed of anything." Gods he was such a jerk. "You're the one who should be ashamed," I retorted, walking away from him. For what, I didn't quite know, but I'd had it with him and his holier-than-though attitude. I didn't need his protection, and I hadn't done anything wrong. Screw him.

So what if I could feel the genuine concern and guilt coming off him in waves. It was like he blamed himself for everything that had happened on the trail. But that wasn't right, and that was his problem, not mine. Honestly, I couldn't figure my old friend out. It was like he'd become a different person overnight, ever since that party at Suki's. I missed my old confidante, but right now there wasn't time to think about it. Getting David safely to headquarters was all that mattered. Well, that, and living through my Dad's upcoming sermon. I just hoped everybody could keep their lips shut about the fact that I'd been kissing a twenty-eight year old.

Otherwise, we might not make it through the evening.

With that in mind, I put on a loose pair of linen pants and a demure sleeveless top with a peter pan collar. I kept my makeup simple, just some blush and a hint of mascara to complete the innocent "Who, me?" aspect of my look. I made a mental note to pick up more beignets on the way home, since sugar was one of my dad's favorite food groups.

I grabbed my satchel and checked on David, who was just hefting his pack over one shoulder.

"Oh, wow," I laughed, eyeing the huge bag. "That's one thing I'm not going to miss about being on the trail."

"But you looked so cute in yours," he protested with a grin. "It must have been half your body weight."

"More, actually. I refused to carry less than my fair share."

Most people carried 60-70 pound packs on the trail. When you were 105 pounds, that suddenly seemed like a lot more. But I'd conditioned myself for the weight, and adjusted quickly to the burden.

"Like I said, adorable." He kissed me on the nose. "You're one of the strongest women I've ever met, and I don't just mean your abs."

"Aw, thanks. I like your abs, too."

I rubbed my hand over his stomach, wondering if this was the last time I'd ever feel them, and gave him a pat.

"Come on, times a'wasting."

As we made our way to the door, Jules came out from her room and gave David a hug goodbye. I could tell she'd been crying, and knew I'd need to make time for her tonight, parental drama notwithstanding. David shook hands with Hollis on the porch. Khai had disappeared into the house, and David didn't ask where he'd gone. There was no love lost between them, that was for sure. Neither seemed interested in a genuine farewell.

Hollis had parked his car on the street, and handed me the keys.

"Don't hurt her."

"I won't." He'd just gotten the sleek silver convertible the year before. It was the first big-ticket item he'd ever bought with his own money, after working in the student bookstore at McGill for the last three years. It was an older model, used, practically an antique at twenty years old, but it was in mint condition. He'd named it Miranda.

Hollis slanted a look at David, his voice going deeper. "Same goes for you."

"Somehow, I suspect I'm the one who's in more danger here," David laughed, trying to make a joke. He was probably right, too. My water powers could do a lot more harm than any of his astral visits. Not to mention anything my brother or Khai could do. Or my father.

Hollis just stared him down with a stony gaze. David's features straightened out of a smile, and he nodded. "Right. Of course. I will protect her with my life."

"I don't think that will be necessary," I blurted, at the same time as Hollis said "Good," and shook his hand. I rolled my eyes at the macho posturing, two men-folk bargaining over a woman's life as if it were their own. It was the sort of millennia-old behavior that would take decades, even centuries, to erase, utopia or no.

"Okay, great, now that you have that settled – I'll see you in a couple hours. If Dad calls before I'm back, tell him I'm playing with rattlesnakes or something. That should keep him calm." I nudged David towards the car, ready to escape the testosterone.

"Two hours? It doesn't take that long to cross the city."

"No, but who know what grand adventures I can get into on the way?" I laughed at Hollis' sudden anxiety, clear both on his face and in his energy field. "Kidding, bro. But I would like to pick up some chocolate and fresh fruit. Maybe check out a bookstore, too."

"Reading? You think now is the time for retail therapy?"

"More than ever. Did you know they have whole sections about empaths and reading energy? I know I'm going to train in the healing arts with Airmed, but I'd like to do some research of my own, too."

Hollis nodded sagely. If there was anything he could understand, it was the value of scientific research. "Okay. That's probably a good idea, actually."

"Don't sound so surprised," I muttered, already halfway into the driver's seat.

"I heard that," Hollis warned. I ignored him and slammed the door on whatever he was about to say next.

David chuckled as the seatbelts slid into place around us both. "You guys are adorable, you know that? I always wanted a brother or sister. You're lucky."

"Lucky? Me? No way. He's such a pain in the-"

"No, you are. He'd do anything for you."

"I guess. He's still a pain, though. So, where are we headed, exactly?"

"The intersection of Rue Ontario East and Avenue Morgan. Gregory's is on the southeast corner."

"Gregory's?" I asked, programming the destination into the GPS before I eased the car out into traffic.

"HQ. Gregory Bank. People think it's a call center, but really it's a research and training facility. A lot of starseeds can't control their powers very well when they first come into them, so Gregory's has facilities in all the big cities where people can stay full-time until they are ready to live on their own again. You'll see."

"Wait a second, back up. So you're saying that Gregory Bank, one of the biggest investment firms in the world, is actually a starseed front? That sounds like some old-world conspiracy theory or something. How could people not know?"

"You have enough money, people don't look too closely at what you're doing. It's easier to hide things. But it wasn't always this way. Gregory's started off as a select council of starseeds, watchers or guardians, I guess you would call them. In Greek, the word was Egregors, and it stuck. After a while, one aspect of the group included acting as a trust for any starseed in need – providing start-up capital, helping them buy land, that sort of thing. Banking with the humans was a natural evolution, and it helped the Gregors finance more starseeds, too. Now that I'm on the warpers' radar, they'll be helping me, too."

"And they help any starseed? That's all they do?"

"It's not as selfless as it sounds. Someone has to make sure that starseeds don't turn into warpers. After the Nommo took off, no one was around to keep an eye on the starseeds, so the Gregors picked up the slack. Proper training in a starseed's early days can make all the difference. Even so, some people can't seem to shake the lure of the dark side. So the Gregors work damage control."

"Damage control?" I glanced sideways at him. "You mean like they hunt down warpers?"

"Not the way you're thinking. Mostly we try to keep regular starseeds out of their clutches. Like back in Vermont. But yeah, if a warper is doing something really terrible, we have people with the training needed to take them down."

"It doesn't sound so different from our Light Guards, I guess. Except, of course, there aren't any Dark fae anymore for them to worry about. Not that you would know that if you ever met Dorian."

"Who's that?"

"The head of the Light Guard. My Grandfather used to be in charge, but he retired after The Flare. Dorian Claffsson took over, and to hear my mom talk about him, you'd think he was missing the old days. He makes sure all the guards are ready for anything, at any moment, and complains all the time about how lazy everybody's become."

"Sounds like the right person for the job," he said, a smile in his voice.

"Yeah, he says 'the tools of light must be protected at all times,'" I mimicked Commander Claffsson's humorless voice.

"We have some people like that on our side, too. I haven't met the team here in Montreal, but I'm hoping at least one of them is that prepared. Based on what I heard in that camp, whatever the warpers are planning must be big."

"So, you said you're going to work for the Gregors?" I asked. "Because it sounds like you could probably just stay there if you wanted, like they used to do with witness protection or whatever."

"I could. But after what I've seen? What they've done to my family? My aunt is devastated, she thinks her baby girl is dead. No. I need to do something. I can't just sit back while the warpers are corrupting innocent people. I'm just grateful I didn't become one of them."

"Me, too," I said. "You know, now that Hollis has called my parents, there's no way the Light Council isn't going to find out. I'm sure they'll keep your people's secret, if they need to, but maybe they can help, too? Like I said, the Light Guard is pretty bad-ass."

"I think you're right. The more help we can get on this... Well, like I said, I think we're gonna need it."

"Good," I sighed. "Because my dad's probably going to want to talk to you, and get a tour of your 'call center' tomorrow. If he can even wait that long."

David chuckled. Of course, he didn't know my dad. If he did, he might not be laughing.

A gentle sound from the GPS reminded me that we were getting close. I scanned the street, and saw the bank up ahead. A state of the art building made of blue mirrors and steel curved like an S along the sidewalk. I'd seen it before, admired its sleek design, but never really paid much attention to it. I imagined that most people felt the same. In a way, it was the perfect place to hide, right in plain sight.

There wasn't any open street parking, so I headed down another block.

"Oh! But you're right across from the Maisonneuve Market! They have the best cheeses there, and the fruits... And the samples. They always have so many free samples, it's great. This couldn't have worked out any better," I said, pulling into an open spot across from one of my favorite places in Montreal. I'd accompanied my mother and Amber to the farmer's market whenever we visited, often touring the gorgeous botanical gardens nearby, too. Otherwise, I wasn't too familiar with this part of the city. I hadn't even known what street the place was on, since I wasn't usually the one driving.

I climbed out of the car and met David on the sidewalk, linking my arm through his. I could tell he was nervous, despite the smile on his face.

We walked towards the building, stopping just outside its doors. It was hard to tell if anyone was even outside, the mirrors reflecting our own faces and the street behind us, rather than the lobby within. The building appeared unguarded, until I noticed two discreet security cameras swiveling to train their lenses on us.

"Do you want me to come in with you?"

"More than anything. But I think I should probably go in on my own. You have enough to deal with right now. If you come in now, you'll probably be stuck in there for over an hour with me, telling the whole story over again."

"Are you sure?"

"Yes. Go, enjoy your market."

"You could come with me," I said hopefully, trying to delay the inevitable as I leaned my head against his arm.

"I'd better not." He turned towards me then, and embraced me, and inhaled deeply against the top of my head, like he was trying to remember my scent.

"Tomorrow then?"

"I'd like that. Maybe you can show me those gardens you were talking about."

"Yes, and we can let the grown-ups talk themselves to death," I said, thinking of my parents, and the sort of people who might be in charge of this cold, glimmering facility.

"Aren't we grown-ups?" he teased.

I blushed. At the age of nineteen, legally I was, of course. I'd had my ascension over a year ago, and every nation in the world considered eighteen the legal age of consent, of adulthood. "I guess. But I've never had to deal with anything like this. I mean, I've never been anything more than just a student."

"Somehow, I doubt that. I know you think I'm a lot older than you, and maybe that scares you, but I promise that I am way more intimidated by you than you could ever be by me."

I laughed, and punched him gently in the shoulder. "Shut up. You couldn't possibly be."

"No really, I am." His face was clear. He wasn't joking. "I mean come on, you're fae. You can make the weather do what you want. You're practically a goddess."

I giggled at the absurdity of the idea, then realized he meant it.

"You're serious."

"Totally."

And then, he kissed me. This time, I could feel his honest interest, like worship, almost. The feeling was heady, prickling along my skin.

Breathless, and knowing that someone inside was watching us, I ended the kiss. "You know, both our ancestors were regarded as gods in ancient times. It didn't do them any good."

"I know. See. There you go, thinking like an adult." He tweaked my nose and adjusted his pack on his back. "Tomorrow, then?"

"Tomorrow," I agreed.

He beamed at me, the summer sun glinting in his hair against the sea of cerulean blue glass walls, then he turned and walked into the mirrored entrance. Silently, the panels slid open, and I caught the barest glimpse of a stark lobby, two guards stationed by the front desk, before the panels slid shut again.

Feeling lonely and cold, despite the sun beating down on me, I shivered.

Chocolate. Strawberries and chocolate. Nothing else would do. Stricken with need, I stalked off towards the market, hoping to fill the sudden hole in my heart.

Chapter 33

You can guess how the rest of my day went. Retail therapy went a long way towards taking my mind off things, but at some point I had to go home.

Once I did, the rest of my day alternated between feeling smothered with love and seriously chastised. And it only got worse when my parents arrived that evening. If I hadn't been practically halfway to Aeden already, I imagine my father would have locked me in my room and thrown away the key for at least a decade. Surprisingly, my mom wasn't much better. She was thrilled that I had discovered my abilities as a water fae, and she did her best to keep my father calm by plying him with chocolate (thank you, Dark Delights at Maisonneuve Market), but the fact was that she was just as upset as my father.

Only after I had promised never to keep anything like this from them again – a promise Hollis and Khai extracted as well – was the family meeting finally adjourned. Feeling totally beat-up, morally and emotionally, I trudged off to my room while the rest of them gathered around Khai's Holo-Cam to check out our trail pictures. At least Jules had stayed by my side the whole time, silently offering support and holding my hand.

Exhausted, I didn't even brush my teeth, just fell into bed and passed out in my clothes for the second night in a row.

And that was exactly how I woke up.

In my clothes.

In the near dark.

At 6am in the morning.

"Seriously? Again?" I moaned at the figure in shadow by the foot of my bed. I pulled a pillow over my head and shut my eyes tight. "Go away."

"Ana, sweetheart. It's time to get up." The bed shifted under the weight of my mother's body as she sat down by my feet and placed a gentle hand on me. "We need to pack you a bag, and Khai's already here."

"What are you talking about?" I asked, pulling the pillow away from my face.

"You went to bed before it was decided. Your father doesn't feel it's safe for you here. He and Bran talked and they want you to brief the Light Council on what you know and start your training in Valhalla immediately."

"Can't it wait a couple hours?" I groaned.

"No. It can't. Khai is bringing you down. Hollis and Dad made plans to meet your friend David in a couple hours, and he wants you safely on your way by then." She sighed. "He's really worried about you, Ana. You know what happened to the rest of your father's family when he was just a child."

I did. His mother and young sister had been slaughtered, tortured at the hands of the Shades. He'd found them in pieces, and it had scarred him for years. Until he'd met my mom. Until her love had healed him.

"But I was supposed to see David today. He won't even know I've gone."

"Look, I'm the last person to lecture you about anything. I was much younger than you when I met your father, and I knew I was in love with him that very first day. But your father... He almost combusted last night when he found out how old David is. Why he cares so much is beyond me, really. I mean, Amber was only 19 when she and Ewan started dating, and he was in his thirties. Age has always been rather meaningless to most fae. But you know how protective he is. I think he'd be mad no matter who you were dating, frankly. And after what you've put everyone through, I think this is for the best right now."

"Seriously?" I wiggled up into a seated position. "What did I do? It's not my fault the warpers had David locked up in the middle of the freaking woods!"

"No," she said, staring at me with a face that said she knew I knew better, "but it is your fault that you hid what had happened from us, and almost got captured by one of these people again later on the trail. What you did was irresponsible, and immature." Real anger laced my mother's voice, a rare occurrence. The worst part? She was right.

"I'm sorry, Mom."

"I'm just glad you're okay," she said, hugging me before she stood. "Now get dressed, and pack a bag, something you can carry."

She left the room and I stared morosely at my backpack. At least this time I wouldn't have to worry about bringing food or bedding.

I changed into some clean pants and a camisole, throwing on a hoodie to combat the morning chill in the air, and packed the coolest clothing I could find, clothes that would withstand the hot, humid weather in Aeden.

In the kitchen, Khai and my parents were sitting around the island picking at the remnants of yesterday's fruit and baked goods. I plopped down onto one of the stools and stuffed a raspberry in my mouth, savoring the sweetness before I spoke.

"What about Jules?" I asked.

"She'll be safe. She's human, and the warpers haven't actually ever seen her, according to what you said. But just to make sure, we plan on staying here for at least a couple weeks."

Jules was going to love that, being chaperoned by my parents. Not.

"And when you leave?"

"By then, we hope to have things sorted out. If need be, she can always stay with Hollis."

I snorted. Apparently, I wasn't the only one keeping details about the trip from our parents.

"What, you don't think Hollis can protect her?" my mother asked, concerned.

"No, it's not that," I laughed. "I'm just wondering who's going to protect him from her."

My parents looked at each other, confused, and Khai spoke up.

"Never mind Ana, they'll be fine. They just had a little misunderstanding on the trail."

"Misunderstanding?" I exclaimed, my voice rising. "He-"

"Shh, you'll wake Jules," Khai said, placing a hand over mine. The heat emanating from it took me off guard. By the gods, he felt like he might combust. I shook my head, trying to keep it clear, to stay focused on what was happening.

"Whatever," I said, yanking my hand away and standing up. "Is it time to go? Because I'm ready."

"Yes." My father picked up my bag and walked towards the door to the basement garage. "You two are going to take Ewan's old Scout. Make sure you park in the new garage at camp and lock it up, Khai. You know how Ewan feels about that car."

"I can't believe that thing is still running," my mother mused. It was an antique thirty years ago, now, it's obsolete. Where does he even find parts for it, Alec?"

"He 3D-prints them," my dad shrugged, as if that should have been obvious. "Besides, the engine's all new, fully upgraded with the latest self-charging fuel cells."

Under the glare of the lights below, the white and yellow 1966 International Scout gleamed. Honestly, every time I saw it, the vehicle seemed younger with age, in better condition than before. Khai grinned, the way boys do when they see a cool car, and I couldn't help but smile.

I turned to my dad, hugging him goodbye.

"I'll miss you, sweet pea. Stay safe down there, and try not to worry. We'll take care of all this. Everything's gonna be fine."

"Thanks, Dad. Be nice to David, okay?"

He grunted, which I took as a yes.

Before I had a chance to realize he'd let me go, my mother was already hugging me, squeezing the life out of me.

"You're stronger than you know, Ana. Unshakeable. I know you've always felt like Hollis shone brighter than you, but you have to know, it was never true. You were perfect, just the way you were, and you're perfect now. You'll always be my shining star." She kissed me on the cheek. "Give Airmed a kiss for me, okay?"

"Okay, I will. I love you, Mom."

"I love you, too, baby," she said, brushing a stray curl of hair away from my face. "Now go, before your father starts crying."

"Hey!" he protested, and she started laughing, pushing him back up the stairs towards the loft.

I got in the car and smiled, watching them disappear from view as Khai backed out of the garage. As much as I'd like to stay mad at them, at my father especially, I couldn't. I loved them too much, and, worse, I could feel how much more they loved me.

This whole water-empath thing was proving to be a real damper on my anger. At least I still had Khai.

I was pretty sure I could stay mad at him for at least another couple days.

Chapter 34

Scratch that.

I couldn't stay mad at Khai for even five minutes.

By the time we were almost out of the city I couldn't take it anymore. I threw up my shields as best I could and waded into conversation at a full tilt.

"Jesus, Khai, I would have thought you'd be gloating right about now, not feeling all mopey and concerned. What gives?"

He looked at me surprised, and then focused on the road.

"I don't know what you're talking about."

"Um, hello, water fae? I can feel what you're feeling. At least, I could. Don't worry, I've thrown up my shields – you were kind of bumming me out, to be honest."

He smirked. "Yeah, right, I bet."

"No really. Your pain is my pain," I intoned, making a face.

"Well, don't worry, I'm over it. I guess I was just feeling sorry for you, getting sent below like this and all. It must suck to have everyone so worried about you."

"It's mildly annoying," I agreed. "But it's nothing I'm not used to."

"Listen, about David, I'm sorry about before, how I acted. If you really like him, that's great. I'm happy for you guys."

I snorted. "Like it matters. I'm pretty sure I'll probably never see him again. I mean, by the time I get back..." I trailed off. "I have a feeling dealing with the warpers is going to be a lot more trouble than anyone thinks. Someone like me would just be in the way."

"What do you mean, someone like you?" he asked, surprised.

"I don't know. Young, I guess? Weak? I'm no warrior."

Khai slammed his hand on the wheel and I jumped. "Gods, are you serious? Why do you always go there? You have just as much training as Hollis, or me, or anyone. You're fae, Ana. Even without your powers, you were one of the strongest people I knew."

"You said I was short."

"You are short. You'll always be short."

"Then why have you been acting so worried about me?"

"I don't know. It's what I do, I guess. Hollis and I were always supposed to be looking out for you when we were kids and you'd tag along, so I guess it became a sort of habit. But it has nothing to do with how capable you are, or aren't. Your height, your powers. None of those things change who you are. What you are. It wasn't David who saved you in the woods, twice. Remember that."

"I guess," I said, chewing my lip and looking out the window.

"I mean it, Ana. You're special, strong. Think about what I've said, okay?"

"I will," I said in a quiet voice, watching the trees pass in a blur.

And I did. Think about it, I mean. I thought about what he'd said the whole ride away from Montreal, following the highway north towards the closest portal to Aeden.

I knew he was right, my mom was right. I was stronger than I'd believed. I had saved David. I'd saved myself. But a part of me still felt much smaller than I was.

Being a water fae, so vulnerable to the feelings of others, didn't make me feel invincible. It made me feel weak. I could only hope that Airmed, the greatest healer of the fae, would have a remedy for what ailed me.

"We're here."

Khai's smooth voice jolted me out of my thoughts. I hadn't even noticed when we'd turned off the main road, which was saying something. The primitive track leading through the privately-owned land surrounding the portal had always been rough and unpaved.

I looked around, noting the relatively new and large log cabin standing strong among the firs, an even larger garage looming before us. Garage might not even have been the right word. Air hangar? The building was massive, a nod to the increased traffic of both fae and humans between Aeden and Midgard, one of many old names for the earth's surface. Since the fae had come out of hiding thirty years ago, there was no reason to hide the portal, or our coming and going. Many portals had evolved into small villages, waystations between Aeden and Midgard. Here, deep in the wild north of Canada, there were fewer visitors, so things were evolving more slowly.

Khai got out, opening the garage door with a key on Ewan's keychain, and came back to park the car. There was ample space within the massive building, but she'd have good company here – Khai parked her between a small solar EV8 all-terrain vehicle and a trio of silver hover-cycles. In the next row over, there was an old Chevord pickup, two older EV6s, and a dirt-bike covered with, what else, dirt.

He opened my door and grabbed my pack, slinging it over his shoulder where it hung awkwardly with his own duffel. It was the first time I had noticed that he had a bag, too.

"You're staying in Aeden?" I asked. "What about that leadership conference. Isn't it coming up in a week or two?"

Khai had scored a coveted teacher's assistant position for the next two years with his advisor, but it meant he had to attend a two-week program at the school. Designed for the best and the brightest, the conference was packed with brilliant speakers and exercises designed to instill good leadership values among its attendees.

Hollis had gone last year, and I had to admit it seemed to have tempered some of his natural arrogance.

"Yeah, I'm not going." He helped me out of the car and walked out into the sunny clearing, locking the garage behind me.

"What do you mean you're not going? It's an amazing opportunity, you have to go," I said, scrambling behind him.

"I'm not going," he said with a shrug. "After everything that's happened, I've decided that I want to focus on other things."

"Like what?" I asked, astounded. Khai had always been fascinated with how things fit together, and engineering was a natural extension of that. Being part of this program would guarantee him his pick of positions after he finished school. And he was giving it up?

"Like, protecting people. Protecting you. I've always enjoyed training to fight, but I never thought it could actually have a purpose, you know? The world seemed so safe, I figured it was a waste of time. I had no idea people like the warpers even existed. But now... I talked to Alec and he said-"

"You talked to my dad?"

"He said he'd arrange for me to train with the Light Guard."

I stared at him, speechless.

"What? It's not like I'm dropping out of school. I'm just going to get some extra training down below. Will you stop staring at me like I've grown another head? I need to do this."

"Fine." I could feel that he meant it, that he was determined and sure. Me? I was confused. Had I ever really known Khai? I hadn't seen this coming at all.

Khai, the warrior.

Sure he was a great fighter, but I'd never imagined he would try to make it his life. Practically every faeling wanted to join the Light Guard, but he hadn't talked about doing that in over a decade. I felt like we'd drifted a thousand miles apart.

"Hey, don't look so sad," he said, smiling. "At least we can hang out, so you won't be all alone with Airmed all the time. I'll even promise to show you any super-secret moves they teach me."

I laughed. "I don't think they have any super-secret moves, at least, not any our parents haven't already taught us."

"True," he laughed. His chat rang and he tapped it, his face instantly sobering up. "Yes, hello, sir."

He held up a hand, gesturing for me to wait, and walked a few steps away. Bored, I looked around. The woods here were older than on the Long Trail, the trees wide and blocking out the sky above, the undergrowth practically non-existent. A familiar stand of boulders loomed nearby, and I knew that we were almost to the caves. Almost to the miles-long tunnel, the portal that would take us down to Aeden, to the realm of the fae.

A sharp pang of alarm surged through me, and I turned towards Khai. Something was wrong.

"Everyone, sir? You didn't see anyone?"

"Khai, what's wrong? What's going on?"

He turned away, ignoring me. "Okay. I understand. You don't have to worry, I promise. I'll take care of her."

He ended the call and swore, swiveling to face me.

"What's happened? Khai? You're freaking me out."

And he was. The emotions coming off him were not good. I felt pain, and fear, and worry. And again – that determination.

"Khai?"

"That was your dad. Him and Hollis went to Gregory's Bank, to the headquarters, and they're gone. Everybody."

"The starseeds cleared out?" David had left without telling me? I couldn't believe it.

"No, I mean- They're gone. The place is a wreck, it's been totally trashed, all the records taken, everything. It looks like the starseeds put up a fight, but they're gone."

"I don't understand. What are you saying?"

"The warpers, Ana. It looks like they hit fast and hard. They've taken everyone."

"David?"

"He's gone, too."

My mind reeled. "We have to go back. We can help find them."

"No, Ana-" he took a step toward me, like a rider of Roumkivara approaching a wild fleet, "we can't. Your father wants you down below, now. He made me promise you'd be safe."

"Safe?! Screw that. We have to go."

"Ana," he placed a hand on my arm, pleading. "Please."

"No!" I screamed, wanting him off me, now. All my anger and anxiety went into that word, creating a shockwave that knocked us both off our feet, flying backwards away from each other.

I recovered first, scrambling to my feet, and I started to run. If Khai wanted to go hide in Aeden, that was fine, but I was going to find David. I would *not* let him get mind-warped.

"Ana! Wait," Khai yelled, following me, and I stopped.

"Will you help me?" I asked.

"I can't. I told you, we have to-"

"Then stay here." I started to move away, and I felt the air crackle around me with static.

"Please, don't make me do this, Ana," Khai cautioned. I ignored him, and took another step. My skin prickled in warning, then everything flared white hot, pain searing through me as my limbs went rigid and I fell, the air around me whispering an apology.

Epilogue

Three days. I've been a prisoner for three days. More, if you count the time I spent knocked out and tied up on the back of Khai's gravicycle, speeding through the air towards Valhalla.

I haven't spoken to Khai since then, although he's been talking to me plenty. I have nothing to say to him.

What would you say to the man who tased you in a bid to keep you "safe?"

Right. Exactly.

I'm free to wander Airmed's home and grounds, but if I try to leave? Let's just say that water fae can create stationary shockwaves, too, and Airmed is one of the best at shielding techniques. Someday, she says, she'll teach me how, but not until she's sure I've come to my senses.

So, I'm stuck here.

My mother calls every night, I hear Airmed talking with her, but I won't speak to her. Right now, my voice, or lack of it, seems to be my only weapon. My one form of protest.

But I hear them. David's still missing. Mialloch and Dorian have both come by, representatives of the Light Council and its Guard. I told them everything I knew, and it didn't feel like nearly enough. I can't shake the feeling that Mialloch knows more than he's telling me. Yesterday a meeting was finally arranged with the Gregors in Boston, but from what I've heard, trust levels are low.

I can't imagine why.

Everyone needs to work together, to save all those people who were taken. First, though, the fae and starseeds have things to discuss. Plans to make. They need to figure out just how they can help each other, what the other side can and cannot do.

Every hour that passes here makes me want to scream. How long before David gets brainwashed, before he becomes a warper?

Is he one of them already?

I can't just sit here and wait. I can't.

Which is why, this evening, I've made a decision. I'm going to let Airmed train me. I'm going to smile and cooperate. I'm even going to forgive Khai. He's been offering to show me some new sparring moves: it turns out that we didn't already know everything, after all, and Khai wants to teach me what he's learning.

So, I'm going to let him. It's what friends do, right?

I'm a quick study, and I can see that I still have a lot to learn.

And then, I'm going to break the hell out of here.

THANK YOU!

We hope you enjoyed book one in the Full Disclosure series! Don't forget to leave a review on Goodreads or Amazon – more than anything else, it's the best way to help support your favorite authors.

Want to See How It All Began?

Discover what it was like to be a Starseed before the world changed – start reading **Song Walker**, the first book in the *Starseeds* series.

Or, check out **Shades of Valhalla**, Book One in the **Inner Origins** Series, and meet Siri and Alec before they saved the world. It's FREE everywhere e-books are sold!

About the Author

Ellis Logan lives a quiet life in New England, obsessing daily over superheros and the gods of old. She spends her days corralling wild children and communing with fairies. When everyone is settled down and the owls begin to sing, you'll find her typing away and munching on dark chocolate while unseen spirits whisper stories in her ear.

Follow Ellis on Facebook and Twitter at
EllisLoganBooks

and

Join Ellis's mailing list at EllisLogan.com
to stay tuned for new releases, giveaways
and more!